A MAN CALLED DRIFTER

Ingrid Bjorkman had been kidnapped. But was she just the bait in a trap meant to snare her would-be rescuers? In their long, gunsmoke-filled lives, three men — Gabriel Moonlight, Latigo Rawlins, and the man known only as Drifter — had made more than their fair share of enemies. And when the trio took to the trail, they had two more shooters to back their play: Raven, daughter of Ingrid — and Deputy US Marshal Liberty Mercer, daughter of Drifter . . .

STEVE HAYES

A MAN CALLED DRIFTER

Complete and Unabridged

LINFORD
Leicester

First published in Great Britain in 2014

First Linford Edition
published 2015

A catalogue record for this book is available
from the British Library.

ISBN 978–1–4448–2645–6

Published by
F. A. Thorpe (Publishing)
Anstey, Leicestershire

Set by Words & Graphics Ltd.
Anstey, Leicestershire
Printed and bound in Great Britain by
T. J. International Ltd., Padstow, Cornwall

This book is printed on acid-free paper

1

Dusk had settled over Santa Rosa, New Mexico, and most of the townspeople were home eating supper. Those who weren't were either drinking in one of the many festive cantinas or working late in the false-fronted, wood-frame stores lining Main Street.

Weary riders and creaking wagons came and went. Stray dogs nosed through the garbage behind the cafes, while out in the desert a coyote talked to the moon. Its mournful howling unnerved the cattle in the holding pens near the railroad station. They stirred restlessly, their nervous lowing mingling with the coarse laughter of the whores in the red light district and the tinkling of a piano in the Copper Palace on Lower Front Street.

All in all, it seemed like a normal evening.

But Lars Gustafson sensed it wasn't. He wasn't sure why but he felt trouble was imminent. A short, gray-bearded Swede crippled by arthritis, he stood at the rear door of his livery stable, watching a man washing up at a water trough by the corral — a corral in which a leggy, sweat-caked sorrel stallion was feeding.

Lars started coughing — a painful lunger's cough that doubled him over and warned that death had him in its sights. When he recovered, he spat an oyster into a nearby pile of hay. If the man washing heard him coughing, he showed no sign of it. Knowing the man's past, Lars had a strange feeling that he was at the core of the trouble he sensed was brewing. A hurricane lamp hanging overhead cast shadows across the old hostler's weathered face, accentuating his wrinkled concern.

'You been gone a spell,' he said finally.

The man didn't respond.

'Ridden a far piece too, looks like.'

The man still didn't answer. Finished washing, he grabbed a faded blue denim shirt draped over the fence and began drying his lean muscular body. His back was turned to Lars and the lamplight showed two recently-healed bullet holes below his left shoulder blade.

'See you picked up some souvenirs since you was last here.'

Again, the man ignored him. Known as Drifter, he was unusually tall with big raw-boned shoulders tapering to narrow hips and long lean legs that were slightly bowed due to a lifetime in the saddle. Though a civilian, he wore old Union Cavalry pants stuffed into knee-high Apache moccasins. That wasn't the only contradictory thing about him. His rugged, jutjawed face displayed no sign of gentleness, yet no meanness either — just an ingrained, unspoken toughness which was ruled by a sense of fair play. Life had weathered him. In his mid-thirties, he looked older and his thick unruly black hair was prematurely streaked with gray at the temples. Dry now, he put on his damp shirt and buttoned it up.

'Ate supper yet, have you?' Lars asked.

Drifter shook his head.

'I got me a mess of leftover beans and salt pork I could fire up.'

Again, Drifter shook his head. Though often taciturn, he was never surly and the hostler, who knew him well, didn't take offense. Drifter picked up his black flat-crowned Stetson, set it squarely on his head, turned and faced Lars.

'Could use an answer, though.'

'First I need a question.'

'When's the Sheriff due back?'

Lars looked surprised. 'Thought you just rode in?'

'So?'

'How'd you know Lonnie was out of town?'

'How'd you get to be so damned nosy?'

4

Lars chuckled, took a plug of tobacco from his shirt pocket, bit off a chunk and gave the rest to Drifter.

Drifter slipped the chaw into his mouth and tongued it between cheek and gum. 'Well?'

'Soon as Old Man Stadtlander gets done pulling his strings, I reckon.'

'Must be fun being a puppet.'

'If boot-licking's your idea of fun.'

'Lonnie Forbes don't seem to mind.'

'He's got no choice — not if he wants to get re-elected.'

'Sell your soul for a tin star?'

'It's a living, like any other.'

'More like a pact with Lucifer if Stillman J. Stadtlander's involved.'

'Everything has its price, Quint. You should know that better than anyone.'

Drifter reddened, stung by the hostler's insinuation. He knew what Lars meant and couldn't disagree with him, but that didn't mean he had to like it. He was about to tell Lars to go to hell when he remembered how much he respected the old hostler . . .

and bottling his anger, managed a rueful smile.

'What's so bad about dying, eh?'

'No one's said it better, friend. And no one's dealt with death better than you.'

'Dealt with or dealt out?'

'Both.'

Drifter's fierce gray eyes turned flinty. 'From anyone else, *amigo*, I'd consider that an insult.'

'Weren't meant to be,' Lars said. 'Ain't my nature to insult folks.'

'Hell, I know that,' said Drifter. 'I was just funning you.'

'In that case, when you get done eating supper, come back and we'll partake in some more 'funning'.'

'Another *lesson* in checkers?'

'Fun for me.'

'Not tonight.'

'Got better fish to fry?'

Drifter gave him a stony look.

Unfazed, the old hostler said: 'Well, it ain't none of my business mind, but wherever you're going, don't plan on going too far. Sorrel's fair wore out.'

Drifter eyed the stallion sourly. 'He's lucky I'm not an Apache.'

'Ride a horse till it drops and then eat it? Sounds practical.'

'Selling that sack of meanness to Ida's Steakhouse sounds even more practical.'

The sorrel stopped eating and glared at Drifter, who turned and walked off.

''Least you could do is eat slowly,' Lars called after him. 'Even a deaf mule sprouting warts deserves a rest.'

Drifter kept walking without bothering to reply.

Lars turned to the sorrel. 'Man's sympathetic to a fault, ain't he?'

The irascible stallion bared its teeth, warning the old hostler to keep his distance.

'Mind your manners,' Lars warned. 'Else, next time I'll mix broken glass with them oats.' He limped back inside to his game of solitaire.

2

Drifter entered the busy dining room of the Carlisle Hotel and sat at a corner table facing the door. He wasn't expecting trouble, but keeping his back to the wall was an old habit and old habits were hard to break. They also kept him alive.

A bored-looking young waitress, on seeing him enter, quickly perked up and approached his table with a glass of buttermilk and a flirtatious smile. She had long auburn hair pinned back by a silver-and-turquoise clip, gray-green eyes and lips shaped for kissing. She asked him if he wanted the usual and when he nodded she entered the kitchen and told the cook to whip up a big bowl of oatmeal with raisins.

When she put the bowl in front of Drifter, he pushed it away in disgust.

'I *said* — my usual!'

'This is better for you.'

'I don't want what's 'better' for me. I want a burned steak, fried onions and a mess of well-done hash browns. Oh, and don't forget the chili sauce.'

'You'll regret it.'

'I'll take a pill.'

'They don't work, remember?'

'Never said they didn't work. Said I still get pains.'

'Same thing, isn't it?'

'Doc says I got to be patient.'

'*And* eat the proper food.'

Drifter didn't answer.

'Fine,' the waitress said, irked. 'Suit yourself. But don't blame me when you're out on the trail, doubled over your saddle 'cause you got a hellacious bellyache.' She started to take the bowl away, but he reluctantly stopped her.

'Wait.' He looked at the oatmeal and sadly shook his head. 'Hell of a price to pay for youthful exuberance!'

As he ate the oatmeal, Drifter checked out the couples and weary drummers eating dinner at the other tables. He didn't recognize anybody but one measured look told him they posed no threat and from then on, he ignored them.

When he'd finished his oatmeal, the waitress brought him a wedge of hot apple pie topped by a mountain of homemade vanilla ice cream.

'What's this?'

'Your reward for being a good patient.'

Drifter grunted his thanks, grabbed a fork and attacked the pie.

The waitress watched him fondly for a moment before asking: 'How's that daughter of yours doing?'

'She's cutting it.'

'Must've been a real challenge for her, jumping right from convent school to being a Deputy US Marshal?'

'If it was, she never mentioned it.'

'Doesn't surprise me. She's got sand, that gal.'

Drifter nodded and went on eating.

'You must be awful proud.'

'Of Emily, sure.'

'Of yourself, too. She *is* your daughter.'

Drifter gave a self-deprecating grunt. 'How Emily turned out wasn't any of my doing. The Mercers deserve all the credit. Taught her manners, self-respect and enough confidence so she'd never run scared.'

He sounded ashamed of himself and the waitress, who liked him more than she let on, rushed to his defense. 'Dammit, Quint, when you going to stop beating yourself up over Emily? I mean no one's blaming you, you know — least of all your daughter.'

Drifter shrugged and looked at the melting ice cream. 'Just 'cause a broken leg mends, doesn't mean you won't still limp.'

'Oh, for . . . ' She snorted disgustedly. 'Now you listen to me, Quint Longley. I've known you since I wore braids and I'm tired of hearing you sell yourself short. The Mercers, fine folks that they were, may have raised Emily but it's your blood in her veins. And

11

that counts for plenty. Never forget that.'

Drifter sighed. Thinking about his past relationship with his daughter was always painful. Now, as his stomach rebelled, he pushed the plate aside, took a small tin box from his pocket, got out a pill and gulped it down with his milk.

'Satisfied . . . *doctor*?'

'Someone has to take care of you — if only for Emily's sake.'

He couldn't argue with that. Finishing his buttermilk, he wiped the creamy white mustache from his upper lip, said: 'Reckon you know she changed her name?'

'To Liberty, right?'

Drifter nodded.

'Heard it was out of respect for a female Deputy Marshal with the same name?'

'*Dead* female Deputy Marshal.'

'Then it's true?'

'That she was gunned down while doing her job, sure.'

'I meant, why your daughter chose to

become a law officer?'

'Mostly, yeah.'

'How's that sit with you?'

'Emily's her own woman. Can do whatever the hell she pleases. That's for true,' Drifter added as the waitress smiled. 'So wipe the smirk off your face.'

'I wasn't smirking, Quint. I was just remembering how hard you tried to stop her from becoming a Marshal in the first place.'

'That's different. Changing her name didn't put her life at risk. Now,' he added, 'if you're all through doctoring me, I'd like my check.'

She totaled his bill and gave it to him. 'I get off in an hour.'

'Be long gone by then.'

'What if I took off now?'

'Why would you want to do that?'

'Thought we could go back to my place.'

'Maybe next time I ride through.'

'That's what you always say.'

Hearing her disappointment, Drifter

said: 'Quit wasting your time on me, Amy. Find yourself a fella your own age who's looking to get hitched.'

'Maybe I'd sooner wait for you.'

'Then you'll die an old maid.' Rising, he put money on the table to cover his check and a tip, politely touched his Stetson and walked out.

The waitress glumly returned to the kitchen, where the cook eyed her sourly.

'When you going to learn that you can't compete with a dead wife?'

'What're you talking about? Drifter's never been married.'

The cook smirked, 'Didn't say it was *his* wife,' and returned to his cooking.

3

Black clouds hid the moon and stars that night and it was full-on dark by the time Drifter reached the Bjorkman ranch.

It wasn't much of a spread. Barely big enough to support a small herd of cattle and a few hogs and horses, it was surrounded by desert scrubland that was so flat anyone approaching in any direction could see the ranch house from miles away.

Drifter, as he rode out of the hills and across the flatland, could see it now in the distance — a sturdy three-room log cabin that Ingrid's late husband, Sven, had built several years before he'd been shot down in Santa Rosa.

Normally, Drifter could also see a lamp glimmering in the window beside the door. It was a sight that always warmed him. He liked Ingrid.

15

She reminded him of a married woman he'd once loved and was delighted that Ingrid's heart belonged to his long-time friend, Gabriel Moonlight. He knew she liked him too, and just being around her and her precocious teenage daughter, Raven, helped dampen the loneliness that not only haunted Drifter, but most desert riders.

Tonight, though, there was no light glowing in the window and he sensed trouble. His uneasiness increased as he got close enough to see that the cabin door was partly open and sticking out of it was a — Comanche war lance!

Alarmed, Drifter dug his spurs into the sorrel's flanks. The startled horse hunched its withers as if to buck. Then, as if it too sensed something was wrong, it broke into a gallop. Drifter gave the sorrel its head until they reached the cabin and then brought the stallion to a slithering, dirt-spraying stop.

Dismounting, Drifter drew his cedar-gripped Colt .45 and cautiously approached the partly open door. It was dark and suspiciously quiet in the cabin. But as he went to open the door wider, he heard a muffled voice followed by someone stamping their boots on the plank floor. Sensing that whoever it was, was trying to warn him about something, he moved to the window. But the curtains that Ingrid Bjorkman had proudly brought with her from Norway were tightly drawn, so that not even a crack showed between them.

Drifter returned to the partly open door and reached for the lance. Before his fingers touched it, he felt a prickling behind his left ear. It was a sensation that only happened when danger threatened, and over the years he'd learned to treat it as an omen. So without touching the door, he removed his hat and poked his head inside.

As his eyes slowly grew accustomed to the darkness, he saw a man tied to a chair facing him. About the same size and build as Drifter, he wore a rough-out suede shirt and cactus-scarred shotgun chaps over his old blue jeans. There was something familiar about him, but Drifter couldn't see who it was because the man's head was covered by a flour sack. By his muffled grunting, Drifter guessed he was gagged. The voice also seemed familiar. So did the fancy tooling on the well-worn boots. Puzzled, Drifter was about to identify himself, when the man moved his feet, causing his spurs to jingle.

Drifter squinted and for the first time saw the spurs. They were ornate Mexican-style spurs with long rowel spikes, the points of which had been filed down so they wouldn't rake the flesh of his horse. Suddenly it all came together and Drifter realized the man was his friend, the outlaw Mesquite Jennings whose birth name was Gabriel Moonlight.

About to speak to him, Drifter changed his mind as he noticed the cord that stretched from the triggers of a double-barreled shotgun mounted on the kitchen table to the inner latch of the door. The gun was aimed at Gabe and Drifter quickly realized that if he'd opened the door any wider, it would have triggered the scattergun and blasted his friend all to hell.

Gathering himself, Drifter said softly: 'Gabe . . . Gabe, it's me, Quint.'

Gagged sounds came from under the sacking.

'It's okay, *amigo*. Just sit tight. I'll get you out of this mess.'

More muffled sounds came from the man.

Drifter ignored them. Pinching the cord between thumb and forefinger, he drew his hunting knife and cut the end attached to the door handle, at the same time making sure it didn't lose any tension.

'Gabe, listen carefully to me. Carefully, you understand?'

Gabe nodded beneath the sack.

'When I tell you to, I want you to

throw yourself backwards, hard as you can, so that the chair overturns. *Comprende?*'

Gabe grunted and vigorously nodded under the sack.

Drifter took a deep breath, made sure he had a firm grip on the cord then said: 'Okay — now!'

Gabe dug the heels of his boots into the floor and hurled himself backward.

At the same instant Drifter released the cord.

4

Gabe landed hard on the plank-floor, the chair shattering under his weight.

The noise of the wood splintering was hidden by the roar of the scattergun as both barrels discharged a load of 12-gauge buckshot, the pellets tearing chunks out of the wall directly behind where an instant earlier Gabe had been sitting.

Before the thunderous boom faded, Drifter had already hunkered down beside his friend. Quickly removing the sack, he started untying the tightly knotted gag.

Gabe grunted impatiently.

'Easy, *amigo* . . . easy. This'll only take a minute.'

Gabe gave another muffled grunt that sounded anything but grateful.

'No need to thank me,' Drifter said sarcastically as he finished untying the knot. 'Just give me your word that in future you'll quit pissing folks off. 'Cause having to keep pulling your sorry ass out of the fire is playing holy hell with my ulcers.'

Gabe spat out the gag and in a voice that was barely a croak, cursed Drifter with every cuss word he knew. As he did, he slipped his hands out of the loosened rope and broken pieces of chair and struggled to his feet — or tried to. But he'd been sitting there so long his legs had gone to sleep. His knees buckled and he would have collapsed if Drifter hadn't grabbed him.

'Whoa, steady, *amigo*.' Drifter helped him sit in a chair at the kitchen table.

'W-W-Water,' Gabe croaked.

Drifter picked up a pitcher on the sink, pumped water into it and brought it to Gabe, who drank greedily. Drifter watched him with a mixture of concern and curiosity. Gabe was his only true friend and there wasn't anything he wouldn't have done for him. 'So, how the hell did you get into this mess?' he asked.

Gabe, his thirst finally quenched, set the pitcher on the table and tried to straighten his brains in an effort to make sense of the last few hours. Before he could, a thought hit him and he blurted: 'Raven — did you see her out there?'

'Uh-uh.'

'How about in Santa Rosa?'

'Nope.'

'Dammit! She should've gotten back by now. All she had to do was wire you, telling you to get here fast as possible.'

'Which she did,' Drifter said. 'What she didn't do, though, was say why.'

'That's 'cause I wanted to tell you myself.'

'Sounds bad.'

'Couldn't be worse.'

'Then quit stalling and get to the meat.'

'Comancheros kidnapped Ingrid!'

'Jesus, no!' Drifter felt like he'd been stabbed in the belly. 'That explains the war lance in the door.'

'It's an old trick,' Gabe said. 'Like baiting a snare. If anyone pulls it out it's *adios* for me.'

'Glad I resisted the temptation.'

'Me, too,' Gabe said, adding: 'Look, I don't want to rush you, but I got to find Ingrid. And fast.'

'Sure, sure,' Drifter said. 'When was she snatched?'

'What day is it?'

'Monday — no, Tuesday, I reckon.'

'You sure?'

'Pretty sure. Why?'

'Seems longer than two days.'

'Two days? You been tied up for *two days*?'

'Close to it.'

'Then I better go throw a saddle on Brandy.'

'You'll have to ride to Mexico to do it.'

'Comancheros?'

Gabe nodded. 'No-good hog-sucking sidewinders, they stole everything that walks — the broomtails I was breaking, cattle, even the damned chickens!'

'Don't sweat it. We'll ride double till we can buy you a horse at the border.'

Gabe wasn't listening. 'It's my goddamn fault,' he said miserably.

'How you figure?'

'I should never have left Ingrid's side. White women living this close to Mexico get abducted all the time. I must've been *loco*.'

'Little late for regrets.'

'That's the hell of it. I know better. But I was dog-tired from riding all day and all I could think of was putting my feet up and getting acquainted with a jug of rye. But you know Ingrid. She ain't happy unless everyone's busy and — '

'What did you two fight about?'

'Who says we fought about anything?'

'I do. Now quit stalling and come clean.'

Gabe gave a grumbling sigh. 'Well, if you must know, Ingrid got on me about the plowing. Kept prodding me . . . insisting I get started right away.'

'That must've gone over well.'

'Like ticks up a mule's ass. Told her I wasn't no pig-raising sod-buster and stormed off to grain Brandy.'

Drifter looked incredulous. 'You were in the barn when she was taken?'

Gabe nodded glumly.

'Christ-on-a-cross!'

'I know, I know. Goddamn Comancheros!'

'They must've been watching you from the hills. Saw you go into the barn and made their move.'

'That's the way I figure it,' Gabe said. 'Sneaky bastards, I never even heard them ride up.'

'What about Raven — where was she?'

'Where she always is — off by herself, moping around in the desert.'

'Just one big happy family.'

Gabe, already steamed, boiled over. 'At least I *got* a family! We may not always see eye-to-eye, but it beats being alone, like you, drifting along like goddamn tumbleweed with the wind up its sorry ass!' He was instantly sorry for what he'd said, but before he could apologize —

Drifter hit him.

Gabe went sprawling. He lay on the floor, dazed, waiting for his head to clear.

Drifter stood over him, fists clenched, ready to do battle. Then as his temper cooled, he regretted the punch and offered Gabe his hand. Gabe hesitated and then took it. Drifter pulled him to his feet. For a moment they stood there, warily eyeing each other, not sure how to proceed.

Finally Gabe stopped massaging his chin, said: 'Satisfied? Or do you want to prod this further?'

'Not unless you do.'

'Nope.' Gabe stuck out his hand. 'I know when I've crossed the line.'

Drifter gladly shook hands. 'Reckon we both could use cooler heads from time to time. Hope I didn't bust a tooth, *amigo*.'

'No chance. Hell, I been in so many

brawls, what few teeth I still got are so loose they ride with the punches.'

Drifter chuckled. 'It's hell getting old, ain't it?'

'Amen to that.'

Drifter took out a little sack containing papers and the makings and began to roll a cigarette.

'Thought you said you'd given up smoking?'

'Not true. Said the *doc* said I should give up smoking.'

''Cause it could rile up your ulcers?'

'Close enough.'

'Yet you're still smoking?'

Drifter shrugged, flared the match and lit his smoke from the flame.

'Well, it's your life I reckon.'

'Exactly. So quit being my conscience. I get enough preaching from Emily.'

'I'll bet.' Gabe grinned wryly. 'Lucky for you she's a lawman or she'd be home nagging you all day long.'

'I'd give anything if she was. After pretending not to be her pa all those years, all I want now is to be with her.'

'That's how I feel about Ingrid,' Gabe said soberly. 'If I was to lose her, hell, I don't know what I'd do.'

'That's why I'm here, *amigo* — to make sure that doesn't happen.' Drifter tossed the little sack to Gabe, who began rolling his own smoke. 'So finish what you were saying. What happened after you stormed into the barn?'

'I was feeding Brandy when suddenly I heard Ingrid scream. I ran out to see what was wrong, and there they were — a whole parcel of them, guns drawn, one fella holding a knife to her throat. I tried to reason with him, but the bastard only laughed and said he'd gut her craw to gizzard if I so much as blinked.'

'So they got the drop on you — why didn't they kill you?'

'They were about to when Raven opened fire from behind those rocks.' Gabe pointed at a nearby rock formation.

'One girl chasing fourteen routed a

band of hard-core Comancheros?'

'I know, I know, it don't seem logical. But Raven was smart enough not to show herself, so they didn't know who was shooting at 'em. She also kept moving from rock to rock, making them think it was more than one shooter.'

'Smart on smart.'

'She can also hit a rabbit on the run. And after she'd winged two of them, the leader got spooked and rode off with Ingrid.'

'What about Raven?'

'She stayed hid till they left.'

'I meant, why didn't she cut you loose?'

'She wanted to, but she was too scared. Figured if she made a mistake and the scattergun went off, there wouldn't be enough of me left to bury.'

'She had a right to be worried,' Drifter said. 'I didn't make a mistake and I still almost got you killed. So that's when you had her wire me?' he added.

'Yeah. You and Lat.'

'Latigo Rawlins?' Drifter looked incredulous. 'You put your trust in a hot-headed bounty hunter who kills for the pure joy of it?'

'I had no choice. I wasn't sure if you could be reached or even if you could, how soon you could get here. 'Sides, I've known Lat for years. He's got his faults, sure, but he'd never turn on me. I'd bet my life on that.'

'You might have to. Lefty's a hard man to corral.'

'Don't sweat it. I'll keep a tight rein on him.'

'Be easier to rope the wind.'

'Now you're talking like a dime novel.'

Drifter let that slide and chewed on his lip — a sure sign he was troubled.

'Well?' Gabe demanded. 'You going to tell me what's chewing on you?'

'This whole thing — it doesn't ring true, *amigo*.'

'What whole thing?'

'The Comancheros. I mean why would border trash like that let you live?'

31

'I already told you. Raven started firing — '

'Skip that. I mean later — after they tied you up? Why not just kill you? It ain't only quicker but means they don't have to keep looking over their shoulder.'

It made sense and Gabe had no answer. 'Okay,' he said finally, 'say you're right. What do you figure the reason was?'

'It's just a hunch.'

'Tell me anyway.'

'They *want* you to follow them — or someone does.'

'Why? The bastards know that soon as I track them down, lead will fly. They also know I won't die cheap.'

'All the more reason it's got to be a trap.'

Gabe thought about it then shrugged. 'Look, I ain't saying you're wrong, Quint. But trap or no trap, I'm still going after them. How about you?'

Drifter looked hurt. 'Need you ask?'

5

Raven knew the vast desert scrubland around her home as well as any Apache.

A rebellious, moody girl who ever since her father's death had become a loner, she'd found The Flats — as the wasteland was called — fascinating from the time she was old enough to walk. From then on she'd spent most of her almost fourteen years exploring the desert and learning how to exist in it until she knew every waterhole, rock and *arroyo*. And in the evenings, when the chores were done, she loved to sit on her father's knee happily regaling him with her daily adventures.

That all tragically ended one afternoon when a stray bullet fired by Slade Stadtlander — who with the Iverson brothers was drunkenly shooting up the town — killed Sven as he and Ingrid were leaving Melvin's Haberdashery.

Raven was devastated. She retreated deep inside herself and refused to speak to anyone for months. She also wrongfully blamed her mother for her father's death, claiming that if Ingrid hadn't insisted on buying a new dress that day neither of them would have been in town, leaving the bullet to kill someone else.

The accusation crushed Ingrid. She already blamed herself for Sven's death and knowing that Raven felt the same way only cut deeper. From then on she'd done everything possible to make it up to her daughter. But Raven ignored her and spent all her days roaming the desolate, sunbaked flatland.

Now, as Raven returned home from the telegraph office in Santa Rosa, she saw the lone horse tied up outside the cabin. Not recognizing it and fearing that it might belong to one of the Comancheros, she'd hidden behind a nearby rocky outcrop, waiting for its owner to leave.

Presently, Drifter and Gabe emerged from the cabin. Raven sighed with relief and was about to show herself when she heard two riders approaching. Unable to see them in the darkness, she remained behind the rocks wondering who they were.

Slowly the rhythmic hoof beats drew closer. She squinted, but still couldn't see the riders. She considered leaving the rocks to get a closer look. But if the desert had taught her anything, it was patience. So she grittily forced herself to wait, staying quiet and still, knowing that sooner or later the horsemen would appear.

She was wrong.

Abruptly the approaching hoof beats stopped.

Silence followed — a long uncanny silence that Raven found threatening.

She listened anxiously but heard nothing but the persistent whine of a mosquito hovering by her ear. Guessing the riders had reined up, and wondering why, she grasped the .22 rifle that had belonged to her father, rested the barrel atop the rocks, curled her forefinger around the trigger and tensely waited for the horsemen to appear.

6

Drifter and Gabe had also heard the riders approaching. But unlike Raven, they were familiar with the unique four-beat 'running walk' of a gaited Tennessee Walker and because such horses were rare in the southwest, they figured that one of the horsemen had to be Latigo Rawlins.

But who the hell was the other?

They hadn't long to wait. Less than a minute later the swaggering little Texas gunman emerged from the darkness leading his horse, a graceful, fine-bred gray that stood fifteen hands high.

''Evening, gents,' he said, smiling boyishly. 'Hope I didn't throw a scare into you coming out of the night like that.'

'If you had,' Drifter retorted, 'you'd be lying feet-up in the dirt.'

Latigo bristled. 'Only way that would

happen, Ace, is if your iron had already cleared leather. And maybe not even then.' As if to prove his point, his left hand moved with blurring speed and almost faster than the eye could follow, one of the two Colt .44s holstered on his hips appeared in his fist.

'Whoa!' Gabe said, stepping between Drifter and Latigo. 'Leather it!'

Latigo smiled wolfishly but otherwise didn't move.

'I mean it, Lefty.' Gabe aimed his Winchester at the little gunman's belly. 'Either sheath that iron or get back on your horse.'

'Thanks,' Drifter said, stepping clear of Gabe. 'But I don't need you or anyone else defending me.'

'I wouldn't count on it,' Latigo warned. 'But just so no one can say I got the drop on you, Ace, we'll start even.' He holstered his gun and grinned mockingly at Drifter, who towered over him.

Drifter didn't move or say anything. But his grim-lipped expression told

Gabe plenty and he said anxiously: 'Don't do it, Quint. He'll kill you.'

Drifter ignored him. Despite knowing he couldn't outdraw Latigo, he wasn't willing to back down. 'Make your play, Shorty.'

It was a nickname Latigo hated and he turned white with fury. A small, wiry, handsome man, he was fastidiously neat and dapper. His clothes were hand-tailored, his boots custom-made, and the pearl-gray Stetson covering his sandy-blond curls looked like it had just come out of a box. His gun-belt and pegged-down holsters were no exception. They were made of the finest leather and oiled daily to prevent sun-damage. The Colts tucked in the holsters were nickel-plated and had ivory grips carved with notches representing the men Latigo had killed with scant provocation or remorse.

But deadly and swaggering as he was, it was his eyes that frightened people the most: amber-yellow and devoid of all compassion, they looked misplaced in his boyishly pretty face. Keeping those eyes fixed menacingly on Drifter, he now said to Gabe: 'Should've told me he'd be here. Would've saved me a long ride.'

'Ain't too late to turn around,' Drifter reminded.

Latigo stiffened and a showdown appeared imminent.

'All right you two roosters,' a voice said. 'Cool your spurs!'

It was a woman's voice, educated but packing authority, and as Drifter looked surprised Deputy US Marshal Liberty Mercer rode out of the darkness on a rangy, sweat-caked red roan that looked as if it could run to hell and back.

'Evening, Gabe,' she said. Then to Drifter: 'Hello, Daddy.'

Drifter scowled. 'What in Sam hell are *you* doing here?'

'I was in Deming delivering a prisoner to the court, and ran into Latigo. When he told me about Gabe's wire, I decided to tag along. Well, at least *pretend* you're glad to see me,' she said as Drifter continued to scowl at her. 'It's been over two months since we — '

'Go home, Emily,' her father growled. 'You're not needed here.'

'Speak for yourself,' Gabe said. 'We're going to need all the help we can get to track down Ingrid.'

Drifter ignored him. 'I don't want you mixed up in this, Emily.'

'*You*-don't-want?' she challenged.

'That's right. *I*-don't-want. And I'm your father.'

'And I'm a Deputy US Marshal, in case you've forgotten.'

'How could I forget something that gnaws on me every day?'

'Good. Then you know I've sworn to uphold the law. And no one's going to stop me from doing just that — including you.'

That didn't sit well with Drifter, but he kept his mouth shut.

Liberty turned to the others. 'While I was in Santa Rosa I wired Marshal

Thompson in Guthrie and he ordered me to stay and make sure that Mrs. Bjorkman comes home safely.'

'Suits me,' Gabe said.

'Me too,' agreed Latigo. 'Nothing I like better than a lawful necktie party.'

'There'll be none of that,' Liberty snapped. 'I'll not stand for any vigilantism — and that includes lynching or unnecessary gunplay.'

'What if it's necessary?' Latigo taunted.

'I'll make that call.' Liberty looked directly at the cold-eyed, dapper little gunman. 'We clear on that, *Mister* Rawlins?'

He knew she only called him that when she was riled, so rather than prod her, he shrugged and said: 'Reckon so.'

'Good. Oh, and one final note: I'll back you every way I can while we're in New Mexico, but my jurisdiction ends at the border.'

'We know that,' Gabe said. 'But with any luck, we'll run those half-breeds down 'fore they cross into Mexico.'

'For Mrs. Bjorkman's sake, I hope so.' Liberty turned to Drifter: 'Well, Daddy? You with us or not?'

Drifter looked at his daughter. What he saw made him ache with pride: a tall, slim, attractive young woman wearing jeans and a leather vest over a sun-faded denim shirt with a Deputy US Marshal's badge pinned to it. Her face was tanned by sun and wind and her long light-brown hair — presently tucked under a gray flat-crowned Stetson — shone with sun-streaks. She wasn't city-style beautiful, but with her dead mother's pert nose and golden-brown eyes and her father's wry smile she turned heads everywhere she went.

She wasn't smiling now, though. Instead, there was a tight-lipped, resolute set to her mouth and a defiant glint in her eyes warning Drifter that much as she loved and respected him, her allegiance to her badge came first.

'I'm with you, Emily,' he said quietly.

She smiled, relieved. 'Then I suggest we stop wasting time and go find Mrs. Bjorkman.'

'First,' Gabe said, 'we got to find Raven.'

7

'You don't have to find me,' Raven said, appearing out of the darkness. 'I'm right here.'

'Well, I'll be jiggered,' Drifter said. 'And all along I thought it was the wind whispering to the sand. You're mighty light-footed, girl.'

'Can thank the Mescaleros for that, Mr. Longley. They're learning me to walk like a spirit ghost.'

'Well, you'll have plenty of time to practice,' Gabe said, ''cause the four of us are going after your mom.'

'Not without me,' she said firmly.

'I'm sorry, missy,' Liberty put in. 'That's out of the question.'

'Marshal Mercer's right,' said Latigo. 'Where we're going ain't no place for a young'un.'

'We're already outnumbered,' Drifter explained. 'Having to worry about you as well would be like shooting ourselves in the foot.'

'Then start shooting,' Raven said, '`cause I'm definitely going.'

'And I say you're not,' Gabe snapped.

Raven glared at him. 'You forgetting something?'

'Like, what?'

'You ain't my pa. So I don't got to do one darn' thing you tell me.'

'I'm *going* to be your pa,' Gabe insisted. 'Real soon, too.'

'Not if you don't find my mom.'

The blunt truth stumped Gabe.

But not Drifter. 'Oh, we'll find her,' he promised. 'Don't worry about that.'

'I ain't worried,' Raven said. She glared defiantly at Liberty. 'If you won't let me ride along, Marshal, I'll go by myself. It's probably best I do anyway. I can follow tracks over anything, even rocks, so finding my mom won't raise a sweat.' She brushed past everyone and entered the cabin.

Drifter rolled his eyes. 'She ain't

short on sass, is she?'

'Never has been,' Gabe said, adding: 'I hate to say this, gents, but Raven's right. We should take her with us.'

'Bad idea,' Liberty said.

'I agree,' Latigo growled. 'She's just a damned kid.'

'Who can track a man over rocks,' Drifter reminded. 'Can you do that?'

'Hell, no.'

'Me neither.'

'Mescaleros taught her,' Gabe said. 'They treat her like one of their own.'

'I say we need Raven,' put in Drifter. 'Marshal?'

'Put that way,' Liberty said, 'it does make sense.'

Gabe looked at Latigo. 'We could sure use your gun on this. 'Sides, if nothing else, I reckon you owe it to Ingrid.'

Latigo hesitated. Then remembering all the meals Ingrid had served him over the years and the nights he'd slept in her barn, he said grudgingly: 'All right, I'll ride along. But if Raven acts up — for any reason — you're on your own.'

'That's fair,' Gabe said. 'I'll go pack some grub and then we'll ride.'

'While you're doing that,' Liberty said, 'I'll gather some wood for torches.'

Latigo looked questioningly at Drifter. 'What's your take on this, Quint?'

'On what?'

'Our odds of getting Ingrid back?'

'For true? Slim and none.'

'How about your gut feeling?'

'My-gut-feeling?' Drifter laughed hollowly. 'Jesus, Lefty, if I'd listened to my gut feeling, I'd be a hundred goddamn miles from here by now.'

8

Carrying flaming torches made out of wet branches wrapped with kerosene-soaked rags Drifter, with Gabriel clinging on behind him, and Latigo rode just ahead of Liberty and Raven. Holding the torches low, they lighted the way for Raven as she searched for hoof prints left by the Comancheros' horses.

The tracks were easy enough to spot in the dry desert dirt, but disappeared whenever the Comancheros crossed shallow creeks or stony gulches or flat rocks swept by wind-blown sand.

But Raven never faltered. Clinging on behind Liberty, her .22 rifle slung over her back, she kept her head down, peering on either side of the Marshal's roan as they followed a trail of hoof prints headed for the Mexican border. The little group moved at a slow but steady pace, Raven never uttering a word while she kept her eyes fixed on the ground.

Finally Gabe, frustrated by her silence, demanded to know if she was sure these were the right hoof prints.

Raven shot him a scornful look. 'If they weren't, do you really think I would've been following them all this time?'

Stung by her sarcasm, Gabe started to scold her. Then realizing how upset she must be at losing her mother, he swallowed his anger and said no more.

Latigo wasn't as forgiving. 'Watch your mouth, you little piss ant,' he warned, 'else I'll paddle that sass out of you.'

'Go ahead,' she dared him. 'But remember: while you're paddling me, the Comancheros are taking Momma closer and closer to the border. You want that on your conscience?'

Before Latigo could reply, Drifter intervened: 'What Gabe meant, Raven, was that lots of riders head for the border every day. So how do you know these particular prints belong to the Comancheros?'

'Because,' she retorted, 'one of their horses has a loose shoe on its right rear hoof. It shifts every time the horse lifts its leg, leaving a messy print even a blind hog could see. And before you ask me how I know it's one of the men who took Momma, I saw the same print by our corral next to the plow. Figured that's where she was standing when they first rode up and . . . ' Raven broke off, voice cracking with emotion, and looked away so they wouldn't see her tears.

'Fair enough,' Drifter said gently. 'We'll follow these prints until we find your ma. And we *will* find her, I promise you.' He looked at the others and by their expressions, knew they were all feeling Raven's pain. 'We're all agreed on that.'

They rode on in grim silence, their flickering torches illuminating the numerous hoof prints showing in the scorched red earth.

9

It wasn't long before they reached Columbus. A tiny, sleepy village on the US-Mexican border named after the celebrated 15th-century explorer, it became famous in 1916 as the first place Pancho Villa and his Villistas attacked when he declared war against the United States.

Now, though, a quarter century earlier, it was known only for its swirling dust storms and relentless searing heat. Tonight there wasn't a dust storm, just a bone-chilling wind that blew down the narrow dirt trail that served as the main street. Rock-hard and full of ruts, the street wound its way between a few scattered adobe hovels, a grubby general store and a rundown cantina outside which was tied a prospector's pack-mule.

Otherwise, Columbus looked abandoned — by man and God.

'Looks like we got here too late,' Liberty said as they reached the village.

'We don't know that for sure,' Gabe said, trying to hide his disappointment. 'They could be holed up in the cantina or any of those shacks — '

'Then where are their horses?'

'Could be hid,' Raven said, equally disappointed.

'Hid? Hidden where?'

'I don't know.' Raven slid down from Liberty's roan and looked about her. 'But if I was a Comanchero who'd stolen a white woman, I sure wouldn't leave my horse out where it could be seen — would you, Marshal?'

'I suppose not,' Liberty said grudgingly. 'But even if you're right, wouldn't they be hurrahing it up in the cantina? And unless I've suddenly gone deaf, I don't hear a sound coming from it.'

For a moment they all listened — and realized Liberty was right: other than a light glowing in the window the cantina seemed to be empty.

'What about tracks — that loose shoe?' Drifter asked Raven. 'Do you see signs of it anywhere?'

'No. The wind must have covered up all the tracks.'

'Maybe if you had more light,' Gabe said. Jumping off the rump of Drifter's horse, he joined Raven and held his flaming torch just ahead of her.

The others watched as Gabe and Raven trudged along, heads lowered, eyes fixed on the wind-blown dirt.

Liberty expelled her frustration in a long sigh. 'I hope I'm wrong,' she said to Drifter and Latigo. 'But I've got a bad feeling that we're wasting our time.'

'You figure the weasels have already crossed over?' Latigo said.

Liberty nodded and gazed toward the border. 'Right about now, I'd bet the whole bunch of them are getting pie-eyed in Palomas.'

'Makes sense,' Latigo agreed. 'It's only minutes from the border.'

'They also know they're safe in

Mexico,' Liberty said. 'From US law anyway.'

'But not from me,' Drifter said grimly. 'I intend to follow those lousy hog-lickers to the ends of the earth, if need be.'

'Doubt if you'll have to go that far,' said Latigo. 'Chihuahua's full of hiding places. You just got to know where to look.'

'Gabe will know. He knows this part of Mexico as well as anyone.' He paused as Gabe and Raven returned, both disconsolate, and then said: 'No luck, huh?'

'Not a trace,' Gabe said. 'Damn wind. It's swept the ground cleaner than a new broom.'

'All ain't lost,' Latigo drawled. 'Quint's riding across with you. Figures on backing your play in Palomas.'

'Or any place else that you need me,' said Drifter.

Gabe smiled gratefully at him. '*Gracias, compadre.* I knew I could count on you.'

'Reckon you can count on me, too,' Latigo said.

Drifter's eyebrows arched in surprise. 'Little out of character, aren't you?'

'Just want to make sure you boys don't dig your own graves is all. 'Course,' he added, looking at Drifter, 'if I ain't welcome . . . '

'Never thought I'd say this,' Drifter replied, 'but right now your company's more than welcome.'

'Amen,' said Gabe.

'What about me?' Raven chimed in. 'Don't count me out.'

'Missy, I've already said you can't go with them,' Liberty reminded her.

'Just try to stop me, Marshal!' Turning, Raven sprinted toward a border sign welcoming visitors to Mexico.

Momentarily, everyone was caught off-guard. Then Drifter spurred his horse after Raven. He quickly caught up with her and without slowing, leaned down and scooped her up with one arm.

She kicked and struggled, yelling for him to put her down.

He ignored her and rejoined the others. There he put Raven over the neck of the sorrel and held her still with one hand while he swatted her butt with the other.

He only hit her once but it hurt and Raven yelped.

'Quit fussing,' Drifter warned, 'else I'll give you the paddling that Mr. Rawlins, here, promised.'

Grumbling to herself, Raven obeyed and lay still.

'What do you want to do with her?' Drifter asked Gabe.

The outlaw mulled it over then turned to Liberty. 'I'd be right grateful, Marshal, if you'd take her back to Santa Rosa and hand her over to Lars Gustafson. He'll look after her and she can pay him back by helping out in the stable.'

'Be happy to,' Liberty said.

'You can take me back,' Raven said, jumping off Drifter's stallion. 'But you

57

can't stop me from running away again *or* trying to find Momma. You'll see.'

'In that case, I'll turn you over to Sheriff Forbes,' Liberty said. 'He can keep you locked up till Gabe and Drifter come back with your mother.'

Raven scowled, but said nothing.

'We'd better make dust,' put in Latigo. 'Longer we wait the less chance we got of catching up to those weasels.'

'First I got to buy a horse,' Gabe said. 'We can't keep riding double or it'll wear out yours.'

'We'll pick one up in Palomas,' Drifter said. 'It'll be cheaper there.' To his daughter, he added: 'Take good care of yourself, Emily.'

'I will, Daddy. You do the same, okay?' She smiled at him, a warm smile that was filled with both love and concern for his safety. Then extending her hand to Raven, she pulled the sullen child up behind her.

'*Vaya con Dios!*' After a quick wave, Liberty wheeled her horse around and rode off.

Drifter watched her go. Her departure left an aching hole in his heart.

'Ain't too late to ride with her,' Gabe said, sensing his friend's pain.

'Might be the smart thing to do, Quint,' Latigo agreed. 'You already short-changed that girl a pile of years.'

'Thanks for reminding me.'

'No need to throw a shoe,' Latigo grumbled. 'I'm just stating a fact.'

'A fact that never stops haunting me,' Drifter said. 'But the way I see it, we got one priority right now: that's to get Ingrid back. After that, I reckon there'll be plenty of time left for fathering.'

10

Puerto Palomas de Villa, known simply as Palomas, was a lawless eyesore in the sun-scorched Mexican desert that was a haven for outlaws, 'breeds, border riff-raff and drunks who frequented the bawdy cantinas that never closed.

As Drifter, Gabe and Latigo approached the outskirts they saw a bunch of cowboys riding toward them. Most were drunk and whooping it up, all of them firing wildly in the air as they spurred their horses along the main street.

'Here comes our welcoming committee,' Latigo said.

'Reckon some things never change,' Drifter grumbled.

'Be glad they don't, Ace. Otherwise, life would be boring as hell.'

'Speak for yourself,' Gabe said. 'Me, I'd give anything to get this price off my head so I could settle down with Ingrid and Raven — ' He stopped as more drunken riders galloped past, their shots mingling with the raucous laughter and relentlessly cheerful Mariachi music played by wandering, gaudily-dressed musicians.

'Think I'll run for Sheriff,' Latigo drawled as they rode past the decrepit adobe stores, shabby cantinas and numerous staggering drunks.

'Give me one good reason,' Drifter said.

'I could use this drunken deadwood as target practice.'

'Nothing like wishful thinking,' Gabe chuckled.

'I can see it all now,' Drifter said. 'The city fathers give Lefty a star and a free box of shells and he turns this hell hole into one big happy boot hill.'

'*And* get paid for doing it,' Latigo said. 'Be like living in high cotton.'

The three of them laughed.

Then Gabe suddenly held up his hand, halting them. 'Look! Over there!'

He pointed at a row of horses tied up outside a cantina. Most were saddled, but a few were half-wild mustangs wearing only rope halters.

'Those the broomtails you were breaking?' Drifter asked.

'Damn right! Now if we can locate the rest of Ingrid's livestock, maybe it'll lead us to her . . .'

'First things first,' Latigo said, wetting his lips.

'Easy, *amigo*,' Drifter cautioned. 'You'll get your fill of killing — *after* we find Ingrid.'

'Always hog-tying my fun,' Latigo grumbled. He nudged his horse forward and followed Drifter across the street. They were now outside a large popular cantina called *El Tecolote*. Dismounting, they tied up the horses.

'How do you want to play this?' Gabe asked Drifter. 'Front and back?'

'Seems sensible. Suit you, Lefty?'

'Sure,' Latigo said. 'Just so I go in front.'

'You will — with me,' Drifter said.

Then to Gabe: 'Since the Comancheros don't know us, we'll wait at the bar while you make your way in through the kitchen. That'll give us a chance to see how many guns we're up against — and if Ingrid's with them.'

'And if she ain't?'

'Been asking myself that same question all the way down here.'

'And?'

'So far, I haven't come up with a satisfying answer.'

'I'll give you one,' Latigo said. 'If Ingrid is in there, we wait at the bar for Gabe to show himself, like you said. Then you gun down the weasels closest to her while I take care of the rest.'

'And me?' Gabe said. 'What am I supposed to be doing?'

'You help me finish 'em off. Then you,' Latigo told Drifter, 'get Ingrid the hell out of there fast as you can, so she ain't hit by flying lead.'

'Yeah, and once you get outside,' Gabe said, 'get a room at the Hotel *Cielo* and wait there for us. That way, if nothing else, Ingrid will be safe.'

'Consider it done,' Drifter said. 'But it still doesn't answer your question. What if she isn't there? How does this play out then?'

'We still gun them all down,' Latigo said. 'And then we go rip this town apart, piece by piece, until we find her.'

Drifter and Gabe exchanged uneasy glances.

'If you got a better plan,' Latigo said, 'spell it out.'

'I don't,' Drifter said.

'Me neither,' added Gabe.

'Then what's chewing on you?'

'Ingrid.'

'What about her?'

'What if she *is* somewhere else — with guards watching her — and they've been ordered to kill her if they hear gunshots?'

'Then she's dead,' Latigo said coldly. 'I won't be happy about it, any more than you will, but this is our only chance. 'Cause if you're right and they got her holed up somewhere, soon as they know we're looking for her, they'll kill her anyway.'

He was right and Drifter and Gabe knew it.

'Okay,' Drifter reluctantly agreed. 'We'll follow Lefty's plan.'

They drew their guns and made sure they were fully loaded before re-holstering them. They then fanned out and marched across the street to the cantina. There, Gabe left them and hurried down an alley that led to the rear of *El Tecolote*.

Drifter and Latigo gave him a few moments to get into position and then they pushed in through the front door of the noisy, smoke-filled cantina.

11

Inside, *El Tecolote* was packed to the walls. A big stuffed owl, after which the cantina was named, peered down from its perch above the bar, its glass eyes reflecting the light of the kerosene lamps hanging from the smoke-stained beams.

Most of the men crowded along the bar were drunk and had big-breasted, skimpily-dressed whores snuggled against them. The bartenders kept the tequila flowing and the cajoling whores made sure the money kept flowing — even if they had to steal it from the pockets of the drunks.

Drifter and Latigo paused at the end of the bar and looked around for Ingrid.

'Can you see her?' asked Latigo, who even on tiptoe couldn't see past the crowd of rowdy customers.

Drifter shook his head.

'What about Gabe?'

Drifter looked toward the door that led to the kitchen and again shook his head.

'I can't see any Comancheros, either. The men at the bar are just *gringo* saddle-warmers down here to chase the rabbit.'

'Then we're wasting time,' Latigo said. 'Let's round up Gabe and try our luck in another cantina.'

'First, let's see if anyone here owns those broomtails outside.'

'Why? We're looking for Ingrid, not a horse thief.'

'Maybe he's not a thief. Maybe he bought the horses from the Comancheros.'

'So?'

'So he might know them. Might even know where they are — ' He broke off as a fight erupted between the two men beside them, one man getting in the first punch that knocked his adversary into Latigo. The dapper little Texas

67

gunman stepped back and kicked the drunk's feet out from under him, sending him sprawling.

'W-Why you m-miserable little runt,' the drunk yelled, struggling to his feet. 'I'll k-kill you for that!' He clumsily went for his gun — then froze as he stared at the Colt .44 that almost magically leaped into Latigo's left hand.

Latigo grinned, a sure sign that he intended to kill the drunk.

Before he could, Gabe elbowed his way through the crowd and pistol-whipped the man across the head. The drunk collapsed, gun dropping from his limp fingers.

'Sorry,' Gabe said as Latigo fumed. 'But he's the brother of the owner of this rat-hole and killing him would just bring more trouble down on us.'

Latigo, still itching to kill the drunk, didn't move.

'You heard Gabe,' Drifter said, grabbing his arm. 'Let's get the hell out of here. C'mon, dammit,' he said when Latigo jerked loose and faced the angry crowd closing in on them. 'Get moving!'

'Nobody calls me that and lives,' snarled Latigo. 'You two want to go — go!'

'Fine,' Drifter said. 'I never try to reason with a fella with a death wish.'

'He's right, Lefty,' Gabe insisted. 'Even you can't kill everyone — not before one of them guns you down.'

Latigo stubbornly stood his ground for another moment. Then realizing they were right, he grudgingly followed Drifter and Gabe outside. There, his temper didn't improve. 'After this is over,' he vowed, 'I'm coming back to gut-shoot that no-good drunk! And nothing you two can say will make me change my mind!'

'Once we've found Ingrid,' Gabe said, 'we won't even try.'

'Fact is,' Drifter added, 'we'll give you our blessings.'

'I'll hold you to that,' Latigo said, still steamed. 'Don't think I won't!'

12

The three of them went from one crowded, rowdy cantina to another, each time staying only long enough to make sure neither Ingrid nor the Comancheros were there before moving on to the next.

'That's it,' Gabe said when they reached the end of the dirt street that ran through the center of Palomas. 'Only places left now are the dives and opium dens down in the *barrio* — and the best of those are worse than scabs on a rattler!'

'Never mind the dime-novel descriptions,' Drifter barked. 'Just tell us where to look next!'

'Wish the hell I knew,' Gabe said wearily.

'What about the Hotel *Cielo*?' Latigo suggested.

'Forget it. I've spent a few nights

there myself and it's mostly drummers, businessmen and rich Mexican ranchers cheating on their wives.'

Stumped, the three of them stood there in the street, across from a livery stable, surrounded by drunken cowboys whooping and firing their guns in the air.

'Dammit, she's got to be somewhere,' Drifter growled.

'Yeah, and someone's got to have seen her,' Gabe said. 'Hell, down here a white woman pretty as Ingrid is going to stick out like a sour note — '

He stopped as in the stable opposite them voices started yelling angrily at each other and within moments, a young trail hand and a half-naked Mexican girl came running out. Both were covered in straw and trying to button up their clothes as they ran — while behind them charged the hostler, a large hulking man holding a shotgun. He paused as he reached the open door and fired in the air, causing the panicked couple to run even faster.

'*Puta!*' he yelled after them. '*Mantengase alejado de mi establo!*'

'Shades of my youth,' Drifter said wistfully.

'Amen,' Gabe echoed.

'You know, *amigo*, there's something I could never figure out.'

'Like, what?'

'Why hostlers spread all that soft, warm, inviting straw in their loft if they plan on kicking your ass out for using it.'

Gabe chuckled. 'My pa had an answer for that.'

'Tell me.'

'Morality, he used to say, is delivered best by a pitchfork.'

Drifter faked a grimace. 'Ouch.'

Latigo wasn't amused. 'No girl I ever met was worth dying for. And that goes double for whores.'

'What's wrong with whores?' Drifter said. 'You pay 'em and they give you what you want — sex, whiskey, a shoulder to cry on — all with no strings attached.'

'They don't ask questions, neither,' Gabe said. 'They don't give a hoot if you're a banker or a bank-*robber*, they treat you just the same — '

'Hold on,' Drifter interrupted. 'What did you just say?'

'That whores treat you — '

'No, no, before that — about whores not giving a hoot if you're a — ?'

''Banker or bank-robber',' Gabe finished. 'What're you driving at, Quint?'

'Ingrid,' Drifter said. 'Reckon I've just figured out where they're holding her.'

'Where?'

'A whorehouse!'

'That sure narrows it down,' Latigo said. 'Palomas is the goddamn capital of whorehouses!'

'I know that, Lefty. What's worse: If I'm right and she *is* in a whorehouse in the hands of those bastards, we got to find her, *muy pronto*!'

'So the question is,' Gabe said, 'if I'm a Comanchero and I got this beautiful white woman with me, which whore-house would I take her to?'

'Why take her to any?' queried Latigo. 'Why not set up camp some-where and just pass her around? That'd keep everybody happy.'

'If that's all they wanted to do,' Drifter said, 'they wouldn't have wasted time crossing the border. They would've stayed in Columbus. Nobody would bother them there. No, those bastards wanted something else.'

'Like, what?'

'I don't know. Just like I don't know why the 'breeds wanted Gabe to follow them. But I definitely think they're connected somehow. I just can't figure out how or who's behind it.'

By their dour, tight-lipped expres-sions, neither could Gabe or Latigo.

'Surely you must have some idea,' Latigo said, 'else you wouldn't have asked Gabe about whorehouses.'

'It's a hunch more than an idea,' Drifter said. 'And I could easily be wrong. In fact I *hope* I'm wrong. But

74

my gut says I'm not and since we don't have any place else to look — '

'Consuelo's!' Gabe exclaimed. 'That's where I'd take her.'

'Why there?'

''Cause Consuelo's an old pro who's done it all. She was a whore herself for years. Then when she got older, she became a madam — a pretty famous one too. Hell, she once told me that she and her girls had been run out of every border town from here to El Paso — which is why she ended up here in Palomas.'

'Keep talking.'

'Well, most towns in Mexico are corrupt as hell. But compared to Palomas, they're like monasteries . . . which makes it paradise for Consuelo. She bribes everyone who could shut her down — the local constables, the *federales, rurales,* politicians — by giving them free sex whenever they want. And then she hires whores who never say no, no matter how depraved the customer is.'

'Gabe's right,' Latigo agreed. 'There ain't nothing those whores won't do — or so I've heard,' he added quickly.

Drifter and Gabe ignored the slip-up. The three of them swapped concerned looks, the idea of Ingrid being abused in any way making them sweat bullets.

'You've convinced me,' Drifter said grimly. 'Lead the way.'

13

Ironically, Consuelo's whores plied their trade in a 200-year-old abandoned monastery just south of the main street. Whether this was by chance or Consuelo's deliberate attempt to thumb her nose at religion no one knew or cared; at least, not if they were men. Most of them gleefully visited the monastery whenever they had the opportunity and money to burn.

Time and the harsh environment had badly damaged the once-elegant adobe building. Its walls were crumbling, the roof leaked and long ago the bell had been removed from the bell-tower to make spittoons.

Inside, crude cubicles occupied every inch of available space — except for the altar. Here, a pile of rubble from a collapsed wall now occupied the area where monks once prayed for the sins of others. Each cubicle had four blankets hanging from the beamed ceiling and contained only the bare necessities: a cot, *serape*, a table on which sat a bottle of tequila, two earthen mugs, and a glass timer half-filled with sand. The timer was turned over by each whore upon entering, telling their customer exactly how many minutes he had to satisfy himself.

When the girls weren't on their backs, working, they sat out in front of the monastery on old, dilapidated rocking chairs, smoking cheap cigarillos, skimpy dresses pulled above their bare knees, legs spread apart, flaunting their wares. They taunted every man, *gringo* or Mexican, who passed by, offering to pleasure him in any way he chose and insulting his manhood if he ignored them.

Tonight, as Drifter, Gabe and Latigo rode up to the monastery there were only two whores sitting out front and they were arguing in Spanish. Reining up a short distance from them, Drifter dismounted and pointed at several saddled horses tied up alongside the monastery.

'Recognize them?' he asked Gabe.

'They're not Ingrid's if that's what you're asking.'

'Comancheros?'

'Could be.'

'Mean you never saw their horses?'

'Uh-uh. The bastards were already on foot when I came out of the barn and I was tied up in the cabin with a sack over my head when they rode off.'

'Even if those aren't their horses,' Latigo said, 'that don't mean they're not inside . . . or that they didn't hide Ingrid's livestock around in back.'

'Only one way to find out,' Gabe said, adding: 'Why don't you two keep the women occupied while I go look?'

Latigo shook his head. 'You speak Mex better than us. I'll go.'

Drifter grabbed his arm, saying: 'First, I want your word, Lefty.'

' 'Bout what?'

79

'That if Ingrid's livestock is back there or you see anything that tips you off the Comancheros are inside, you'll keep your irons sheathed and get back here, *muy pronto*!'

'Sure,' Latigo said. 'If that's the way you want to play it.'

'It is. The only hope we got of rescuing Ingrid is by surprise. And I don't want your love of killing to end that hope.'

Latigo looked indignant. 'Don't throw a shoe, Ace. No matter what you've heard, I don't shoot everybody on sight.' He hurried away.

'For Ingrid's sake,' Drifter said grimly, 'I hope he means that and doesn't go off half-cocked.'

'If I was a gambler,' Gabe said gloomily, 'that's one bet I wouldn't take.'

14

After giving Latigo enough time to reach the rear of the monastery, Drifter and Gabe stubbed out their smokes and led their horses toward the two young whores sitting in front of the big cathedral-shaped door. They were still arguing and didn't notice the men approaching.

'What're they fighting about?' Drifter asked. 'They're jabbering so fast I can't make it out.'

'The older one's accusing her cousin of stealing her last customer,' Gabe said. 'And the cousin's denying it.'

The whores suddenly noticed the two *Norteamericanos* approaching. They immediately stopped arguing and, all smiles, beckoned to them.

'Whatever you tell 'em,' Drifter said softly so only Gabe could hear, 'make sure you stall long enough for Latigo to get back to us.'

'That may be harder than you think,' Gabe replied as the whores invitingly lifted up their dresses, baring themselves. 'Right now I don't figure these girls have 'no' on their mind.'

'Well, you'd better think of something, *amigo* — and fast — because if there *are* Comancheros inside and they hear us arguing with these whores, they're going to come boiling out, looking for a fight, and then — '

'I know, I know,' Gabe said. 'Ingrid's days are numbered.'

'Ours too, most likely.'

'Reckon I could always haggle over the price.'

'Fine. Just drag it out.'

They'd reached the two whores. As the girls rose to greet them, Gabe asked them in Spanish how much they charged for sex.

'*Cinco pesos, señor,*' replied the older whore, who looked about sixteen.

Gabe shook his head. 'No, no, too much.'

'*No comprende, señor.*'

'*Demasiado.*'

'*No, no, señor. No demasiado.*'

'Keep at it,' Drifter said as Gabe paused. 'You got their attention.'

Gabe smiled at the older whore, said: '*Cinco centavos, señorita.*'

'*Cinco centavos?*' The whore looked at her cousin as if Gabe was crazy then turned back to him. '*Usted hace broma, no?*'

'No,' he said. 'No joke. *Cinco centavos.*'

The older whore turned away, disgusted. But her cousin wouldn't give up.

'*Dos pesos, señor?*' she said. No more than fourteen, she grasped Drifter's hand and pressed it over her bare breast. '*Muy bien, señor.* You like much.'

'Sure I like,' Drifter said, removing his hand. 'But not two *pesos*' worth.'

'They're not going for it,' Gabe said as the whores seemed ready to leave. 'I better up our price or this conversation's going to end quicker than the Alamo.'

'Go ahead. We should hear from Lefty any time now.'

Gabe smiled at the younger whore. '*Cincueta centavos?*'

The whores looked at each other, undecided.

'Uh-oh,' Gabe muttered. 'I think they're actually considering it.'

'Tell them it's for both of us. That ought to twist their nipples.'

Gabe pointed at himself and then Drifter, saying: '*Yo y mi amigo — cincueta centavos?*'

The older whore lost her temper. Spitting at Gabe's feet, she cursed him in Spanish — only to suddenly stop as gunshots were heard behind the monastery.

'Goddammit!' Drifter exclaimed. 'I knew we couldn't trust that trigger-happy little snake!'

'Easy,' Gabe cautioned. 'We don't even know if Lat's involved yet. And even if he is, maybe he was prodded into it — ' He broke off as Latigo came running up the street toward them,

84

both guns drawn.

'They're in there!' he yelled. ''Bout fifty of 'em! Bastards jumped me as I was sneaking out the back door!'

'What about Ingrid?' Gabe said. 'Did you see her?'

'Maybe.'

'*Maybe*?

'I ain't sure.'

'What the hell, Latigo,' began Drifter.

'No, no, you don't understand. They got three women prisoners, all white. But I never saw their faces. One of them *could* be Ingrid, I reckon. She's got pale yellow hair and is about the same size, but — ' He ducked as shots were fired at them, the bullets ricocheting off the wall by their heads. Whirling around, they saw a bunch of Comancheros charging toward them from the rear of the monastery.

'Take cover!' Gabe shouted. 'If they get behind us, we'll be caught in their crossfire.'

'Not if we attack,' Drifter said as the two frightened whores opened the big

85

monastery door and ran inside.

'Attack? Are you *loco*?'

Drifter answered by vaulting into the saddle and digging his spurs into the sorrel. Startled, the stallion squealed angrily, bucked once then charged straight at the now-open door.

Gabe and Latigo watched as Drifter ducked his head so as not to be decapitated by the top of the arched doorway and galloped into the monastery.

'Crazy son of a bitch,' Gabe cursed as he swung up on the gray behind Latigo. 'He ain't going to be satisfied till we're all squatting on God's doorstep!'

15

The sudden appearance of Drifter as he and the sorrel came barreling through the door panicked everyone in the monastery. Whores and their customers burst out of the cubicles, some cowering, others scattering in fear, their screams adding to the chaos — while the remaining Comancheros, many of them pulling up their pants as they ran, desperately sought cover in the altar area.

Drifter gave them no time to recover. He charged straight at them, reins in one hand, six-gun blazing in the other.

Behind him rode Latigo and Gabe, firing as they came.

Several Comancheros were gunned down as they fled. The others made it to the altar, took cover behind the rubble and returned fire. But most of them were so panicked by the

Norteamericanos' swift attack, their shots went wild.

Drifter leapt from his horse as he reached the altar, grabbed his rifle from the saddle boot and pumped shot after shot into the demoralized Comancheros. Gabe and Latigo did the same. When only a few bandits were left, they dropped their guns and raised their hands in surrender.

Latigo happily shot one of them and was about to shoot another when Drifter grabbed his gun-hand.

'Dammit, Lefty, can't you see they've folded?'

Latigo angrily jerked his arm loose, 'Get the hell out of my way!' and tried to push past Drifter. When he couldn't, he drew his other gun and jammed it into Drifter's belly. 'I swear I'll kill you if don't — '

He stopped as he felt a Winchester press against back.

'Squeeze that trigger,' Gabe said, 'and you won't see sunup!'

Latigo stiffened, hesitated a moment,

then holstered his guns.

By then the Comancheros had fled out the back door.

Latigo stood there for a moment, fuming. Then he turned and faced Drifter, voice trembling with rage as he said: 'You ever play God around me again, Quint, so help me I'll gun you down in your boots.'

'You murder another unarmed man,' Drifter warned, 'and you'll never get the chance.'

Eyes locked, they both seemed on the verge of drawing.

That's when Gabe swung around and aimed his Winchester at them. 'God-*damn* you!' he raged. 'I ought to shoot you both!' His finger tightened around the trigger and for an instant he appeared ready to carry out his threat.

Then regaining control of his anger, he slowly lowered the rifle.

'Next time you see Ingrid,' he hissed, 'thank her.'

'For what?' Latigo asked.

'Saving your sorry lives. 'Cause if I

didn't need you *pistoleros* to help me find her, you'd both be feet up!'

Drifter and Latigo had no doubt Gabe meant it and for once neither of them had anything to say.

Once the shooting was over, the whores and their customers emerged from the cubicles. They stood there, half-naked, fearfully looking about them.

Drifter thumbed at the two nearest whores and told Gabe to ask them where the three white women were. Gabe obeyed. Neither whore answered.

'Ask 'em again,' Drifter said. 'And this time, say I'll shoot them if they don't answer.'

Gabe spoke briefly to the whores. The older one replied sullenly in Spanish.

Gabe turned back to Drifter. 'She says they don't know. Says the last they saw of them, *El Espada* — that's the leader's name — and his guerrillas — '

'His what?'

'Bodyguards — were herding them

out that door over there.' Gabe indicated the rear door of the monastery.

'How long ago was that?'

Gabe spoke to the older whore, who shrugged, then answered his question.

'She ain't sure,' he told Drifter. 'Maybe right before you rode in.'

'Makes sense,' Latigo said. 'They were here when I ducked out to warn you.'

'She also said that *El Espada* gave two of the women to his bodyguards for their pleasure — '

'Which two — did she say?'

'No.'

'Ask her if the woman with the pale yellow hair was one of them?'

Gabe questioned the older whore, who shook her head indifferently and spoke to her companion. She then turned back to Gabe and answered his question.

'No,' Gabe told Drifter. '*El Espada* took her with him — ' His voice was drowned out by a volley of shots fired from the entrance.

The three of them dived for cover, bullets whining overhead.

Unchallenged, the rest of the Comancheros came pouring in through the front door, firing as they advanced.

'Damn!' Gabe exclaimed as he ducked down beside Drifter. 'How come we always manage to outstay our welcome?'

'Shut up and shoot!' Drifter barked. 'Else we won't have to worry about being welcome anywhere again.' Even as he spoke he rested his gun atop the rubble he was hiding behind and emptied it into the onrushing Comancheros.

Gabe and Latigo did the same. Their combined gunfire broke the charge.

The Comancheros retreated, stumbling over their dead comrades as they scattered and took refuge behind the nearest cover. From there they returned fire. Their accuracy was poor, but there were so many of them that the deadly hail of bullets kept Drifter, Gabe and

Latigo pinned down.

Finally Drifter had had enough. 'Cover me,' he told the others. As they began firing rapidly, he crawled to the broken remains of the wooden stairway leading up to the bell-tower. Climbing up until he was high enough to see the Comancheros crouched behind their barricades, he began picking them off one by one, forcing the survivors to scramble for their lives.

The shootout raged on.

Drifter jumped down from the steps and rejoined Gabe and Latigo. At first they held their own. But the odds were so overwhelmingly against them that despite their accuracy, it soon became a lopsided fight. Bullets zipped about their heads, spattering the adobe walls behind them. Gradually the Comancheros edged closer. The bad news didn't stop there: the whores' customers, now dressed and angry at the *gringos* for spoiling their chance of getting bedded, joined the Comancheros.

'Where the hell are the *federales* when you need them?' Gabe grumbled.

'Even if they did show up,' Drifter said, 'what makes you think they'd take our side?'

'Well, someone better,' Latigo said as he reloaded, "cause I'm almost out.'

'Me, too,' Drifter said. Both looked questioningly at Gabe.

The outlaw answered by holding up his near-empty gun-belt.

Drifter shrugged philosophically. 'Reckon we're down to two choices, *amigos*. Brace the bastards head-on or surrender and face a firing squad.'

'I'm not big on surrendering,' Latigo growled.

'No firing squad for me,' Gabe said as he loaded his last six bullets into his Colt. 'I want to see the son of a bitch who shoots me.'

'That makes it unanimous,' Drifter said. He ducked as a bullet ricocheted off the rubble and struck the painted clay crucifix hanging on the wall above his head. It shattered, showering him with broken pieces of the Christ figure. He carefully brushed them off and held up a piece of the cross, his tone somber as he said: 'God knows I'm not the most religious man, but seems to me like this is a good omen.'

Before either Gabe or Latigo could agree — shooting suddenly broke out behind the Comancheros. Caught off-guard, several of them were killed instantly. The rest whirled around to see who the attackers were.

What they saw were a Winchester and a .22 rifle firing at them from the arched doorway . . . the shooters themselves barely visible in the darkness.

Gabe, recognizing the .22, swore softly under his breath.

16

'Hell's fire,' he then exclaimed. 'Raven!'

'And Emily,' Drifter added as he made out the other shooter.

'What the hell made 'em come back here?' Latigo demanded.

'I don't know,' Gabe said. 'But they sure are a welcome sight.'

'Let's take advantage of it,' Drifter said, 'and meet these 'breeds head-on.'

'My kind of thinking,' said Gabe.

'Count me in,' Latigo added, joining them.

The three of them lined up abreast of one another and then strode between the cubicles, gunning down anyone who threatened them.

The Comancheros, realizing they were caught in a deadly crossfire, soon threw down their weapons and surrendered. The whores' customers, who were fighting alongside them, did the same — all but one man that is, who seemed reluctant to drop his gun.

Latigo gleefully shot him in the belly.

'Dammit, hold your fire,' Drifter snapped.

Latigo started to argue; then shrugged and holstered his Colts.

Drifter pointed at the wall to his left and said to Gabe: 'Tell them to line up against that wall.'

'Whores as well?'

'Everyone.'

Gabe faced the sullen, unarmed men and women and indicated the wall with his gun. '*Soporte contra la pared!*'

They all obeyed.

Drifter pried a Springfield carbine from a dead Comanchero's hand, made sure it was loaded and then covered the prisoners.

'Wonder if they would've been so quick to surrender,' Gabe mused, 'if they'd known we were almost out of lead?'

'Not almost,' Drifter said. He drew his Colt and squeezed the trigger, the hammer making a dull click.

'I only had one round left myself,' Latigo admitted.

'Two for me,' Gabe said. He grinned as he saw Liberty and Raven approaching from the entrance. 'Reckon it's time to thank the ladies.'

'I second that,' Drifter said.

Latigo finished unbuckling a gun-belt from one of the corpses before saying uneasily: 'Do you reckon we need to tell them we were out of ammo?'

'Hell, no,' Gabe said. 'If Raven ever found out she'd saved my life, I'd never hear the last of it.'

'Then let's keep it under our hats.'

'Agreed,' Gabe said. 'How about it, Quint?'

Drifter wasn't listening. He was already walking toward his daughter, whom only a few minutes ago he thought he'd never see again. Yet here she was, safely beside him, and he was so overwhelmed with relief he couldn't find words to express himself.

'H-Hyah,' was all he could muster.

'Hello, Daddy,' Liberty said, smiling. 'Surprised to see us?'

'A mite.'

'You don't seem too happy about it.'

'I'm still wrestling with that.'

'Same old Quint Longley.'

Drifter swallowed a lump in his throat. 'You couldn't be further from the truth, Emily.'

'Be pretty to think so . . . ' She paused and gazed about her. 'Looks like we got here at the appropriate time.'

'For that I thank you.'

'It's me you ought to be thanking,' Raven grumbled. 'If I hadn't begged the Marshal to help me find my mom, we'd still be on our way to Santa Rosa.'

'She's right,' admitted Liberty. She fondly ruffled Raven's short black hair. 'She can be awfully persuasive when she wants to be.'

'Raven!'

Raven saw Gabe beckoning to her and trudged over to him.

Liberty noticed Drifter's frown and immediately guessed what he was thinking. 'I know I shouldn't have let her talk me into it, Daddy. But I got to thinking how much I missed my mom after she was killed, and decided Raven deserves better than that.'

'She does. And so did you.'

Liberty laughed humorlessly. 'Like you always say: 'Little late for regrets.''

Drifter nodded, his expression revealing how much he too missed her mother, then said quietly: 'I'm real glad you're here, daughter mine.'

'For true?'

Drifter smiled wryly at hearing another of his phrases. 'For true.'

'Then that makes it all worthwhile.' She looked up at him, her smile healing the hole in his heart. Drifter wanted to hug her. But, like most men of action, he felt awkward about it. Instead he placed his hands on her shoulders and squeezed fondly, hoping she'd understand how much just touching her meant to him.

For a few moments neither spoke; then Liberty said: 'You really did love my mother, didn't you?'

'More than the day is long.'

'Then why didn't you ask her to run off with you? You know she would've.'

'That's not true.'

'Sure it is. Mom and Pa Frank even talked about it once after you rode off.'

'You must've misunderstood them.'

'Nothing to misunderstand. Pa found Momma in the barn, saddling her horse and wanted to know where she was going. When she didn't answer him and wouldn't even look at him, he came right out with it. Said he wasn't going to beg her to stay and knew he couldn't stop her from leaving, but wanted her to know that she wasn't taking me with her. He'd shoot me before he'd let that happen.'

'Shoot you?'

'That's what he said and, you know what? I think he meant it. So did

101

Mother, 'cause she unsaddled her horse, went inside the house and never tried to leave again. But I heard her crying sometimes after you left, so I knew she hadn't stopped loving you. She just couldn't find it in her heart to run out on me.'

Drifter sighed heavily.

'Knowing all that, Daddy, don't you think it's time you told me why you didn't just sweep her up in your arms and ride of with her?'

Drifter said nothing, but his expression was filled with pain and regret. 'Wasn't just one reason, Emily,' he said finally, 'it was a whole gaggle of reasons.'

'I'd still like to hear them.'

He shrugged. 'Not wanting to break up a loving family — or destroy the life of a good man who was a better husband than I ever could be. And most important of all, not wanting to deprive you of a mother or ruin the reputation of a fine woman who later would find out she'd made a mistake.'

'Why would loving you be a mistake?'

'Because I couldn't offer her anything. Worse, I didn't even have the guts to risk trying. I just wanted to steal the honey without facing the bees.'

'So you ran out on her?'

'That's for true.'

'*And* me?'

'Also, for true.'

'Ever regret it?'

'Every second of every minute of every day.'

Liberty was silent a long time as she mulled over his explanation.

'Well,' she said finally, 'thanks for sharing that with me. Now I don't have to lie awake wondering anymore. As for now, I've decided to stay and help you find Mrs. Bjorkman.'

'What about jurisdiction problems?'

Liberty shrugged. 'Crossing the border nullifies my authority as an officer of the law, but I assure you it won't hamper my shooting.'

'Reckon you've already proved that,' he said, eying the corpses. 'Now if you can figure out what to do with this bunch of misfits, my day will be complete.'

Liberty thought a moment before saying: 'Well, even though I don't have any official capacity down here, the US Marshal's office does have a working relationship with the *federales*. If we can locate the nearest garrison, maybe I could persuade the Commander to take custody of the prisoners.'

'We don't have that much time. According to this whore Gabe spoke to, *El Espada* and his bodyguards took off earlier with three white women prisoners — '

'Was Mrs. Bjorkman one of them?'

'There's a good chance of it, yeah. Trouble is we don't know where they went.'

'A hideout?'

'Probably. But, where?'

'What about the prisoners — wouldn't they know where the hideout is?'

'Even if they did, they wouldn't tell us.'

'They might — if we ran a bluff.'

'Bluff?' Drifter frowned. 'What sort of bluff?'

'Follow me. I'll show you.'

17

It was still dark but pale lemon, green and violet streaks were starting to lighten the eastern sky, hinting that dawn was approaching.

Drifter, Gabe and Latigo, their gun-belts now filled with ammo, herded all the prisoners out of the monastery. Outside, Liberty stood guarding six captives who sat on the ground with their backs to the entrance. They were blindfolded, their hands were tied behind them and by their slumped-forward posture it was easy to assume that they were expecting to die.

With Gabe issuing orders in Spanish, the prisoners lined up some twenty feet in back of the blindfolded captives.

Drifter walked over behind the first captive, drew his Colt and pressed the muzzle against the back of the man's head. 'Okay,' he told Gabe. 'Ask away.'

Gabe confronted one of the prisoners standing in line and in Spanish asked him where *El Espado* had taken the white women with the yellow hair. When the man didn't answer, Gabe repeated the question. Again, the prisoner didn't answer.

Drifter promptly shot the blindfolded captive, who slumped forward on the dirt.

'Ask him again,' Drifter said. 'And this time tell him that we know they have a hideout in the hills and we want to know where it is.'

Gabe translated everything in Spanish to the prisoner. The man kept his head down and mumbled something.

Gabe turned to Drifter. 'Says he doesn't know anything about a hideout.'

'That's too bad.' Drifter moved behind the next captive and shot him in the back of the head. His skull cracked open and blood sprayed everywhere as he sprawled on his face.

Every prisoner flinched and angry

murmurs came from them.

'Reckon they're getting your drift,' Latigo said.

'I hope so,' Drifter replied. 'I'm wasting good lead.' Then to Gabe: 'Tell them that after I've shot these six men, another six will take their place. Then six more, and so on, until they're all dead or someone tells me what I want to know.'

Gabe nodded and repeated Drifter's threat to the prisoners. They stirred uneasily, many of them whispering among themselves, but no one spoke up.

Without hesitation Drifter shot another captive.

Gabe turned to the prisoners and in Spanish begged them to speak up before any more of their comrades were killed.

After more urgent whispering, several of the prisoners nodded as if agreeing to something and finally one man stepped forward.

'Hear him out,' Drifter told Gabe.

'And if you figure he's just stalling for time, tell him I'm out of patience and he's going to be the next one to die.'

The prisoner spoke before Gabe could. '*Por favor, señor*,' he said to Drifter, 'No shoot. I say what you ask.'

'It's about time. What's your name, *amigo*?'

'Adelmo Morales, *señor*.'

'Okay, Adelmo, here's what's going to happen: you're going to tell me where your hideout is; then you're going to ride with us so you can *show* us where it is. And if you're lying, *amigo*, I'm going to drag you behind my horse until every ounce of flesh has been scraped from your body. *Comprende?*'

'*Si, si, El Jefe*. But I no lie. You see. I tell truth.'

'For your sake, I hope so.' Holstering his Colt, Drifter turned back to Gabe.

'You and Lat take everyone inside the monastery. Then pick out extra horses for us and scatter the rest so we won't have to keep looking over our shoulders.'

Gabe nodded and waved to Latigo to help him round up the prisoners.

'What about the corpses?' Liberty asked. 'We can't just leave them to rot.'

''Fraid we got to,' Drifter said. 'There isn't time to bury them.' Before she could protest, he added: 'Got any 'cuffs in your saddlebags?'

'Yes. Why?'

'Put 'em on Adelmo, here, and throw away his boots.'

'But if he has to walk or run alongside us, his feet will be cut to pieces.'

'That's the point. Then he can't escape so easily.'

'Daddy — !'

'Now don't go soft on me.'

'I'm not, but — '

'Whose side you on anyway?'

'Yours, of course.'

'I wonder. 'Cause the man you're defending and his whore-loving friends not only may have kidnapped Ingrid Bjorkman — a kind, Sunday-go-to-church woman who never harmed a soul in her life — but most likely all took turns ravaging her!'

'Daddy, stop it — '

'What's more,' Drifter continued, 'the bastards may have already killed her!'

'I'm perfectly aware of that.'

'Are you? Then do like I tell you.'

'Not if it means deliberately cutting a man's feet to pieces — that's inhumane!'

For an instant they stood there, glowering, neither sure what to say next.

Then, 'What about me?' a voice said. 'What can I do to help?'

Drifter and Liberty turned as Raven stepped from behind the monastery wall.

'I told you to stay with the horses,' Drifter barked.

'I did stay,' Raven replied. 'But when I heard all the shooting, I got worried and came to see what was going on.'

'Nothing's going on. Marshal Mercer and I were just talking.'

'What about those men?' Raven demanded, indicating the bodies of the blindfolded captives. 'Were they really all dead — 'fore you shot them, I mean?'

Drifter nodded, inwardly wincing as his ulcers flared up.

'Would you have shot them like that if they hadn't been?'

'Of course he wouldn't,' Liberty said.

'It was just a bluff,' Drifter explained. 'A means of making the men who kidnapped your mother tell us where she is. Now,' he added firmly, 'be a good girl, Raven, and go tell Mr. Moonlight to pick you out a horse. We got some hard riding ahead of us.'

'I don't need his help,' she said, offended. 'I can pick out my darn' own horse.'

'Fine,' Drifter said. 'Then go do it, *muy pronto*!' He waited for her to run off then said to Liberty: 'I don't envy Gabe trying to raise that little she-wolf. Not even if it means marrying Ingrid in the bargain.'

112

Liberty smiled, her anger now spent. 'You've got that backwards, Daddy. It's Raven that's going to be doing the raising. Gabe's just along for the ride.'

18

It took Raven almost an hour to find the loose-shoe hoof print among all the other prints in the dry, powdery dirt. By then the wind had died down and dawn was in full splendor. Puffy pink clouds hung over the mountains to the southeast, while the rest of the pale gray sky was aflame with various shades of red, orange, yellow — all framed by the palest of greens and mauves.

'They're headed that way,' Raven said, pointing toward the mountains.

'They?' Drifter queried. 'Other men are traveling with this loose-shoe rider?'

She nodded. ''Cording to the prints, six of them.'

'Any way of telling how far they're ahead of us?'

'Depends on the wind.'

'Why?' Liberty asked. 'What's the wind got to do with it?'

'Everything.' Raven hunkered down and indicated the hoof prints she'd been studying. 'These are either very fresh — which we know they ain't — or there hasn't been any wind to blow dirt over them. Also, look at the edges,' she pointed. 'They're still — you know, there.'

'Intact, you mean?' Liberty said.

Raven nodded. 'And they wouldn't be if the wind was still blowing. They'd either be all messed up or covered completely.'

'So the question is,' Drifter said, addressing everyone, 'how long ago did the wind die down? Anyone remember?'

''Bout an hour ago,' Latigo guessed.

'More like an hour and a half,' Gabe corrected.

'Longer than that,' Liberty said. 'Maybe even two hours. Reason I know is,' she continued as the others turned to her, 'when we were dragging those corpses over in front of the monastery the wind was still blowing.

But later, by the time we brought the prisoners out and you,' she said to Drifter, 'began questioning them, it had almost stopped.'

'You're sure of that?'

'Positive. I remember seeing all the flies buzzing around the corpses, and thinking — wishing that the wind would start up again and blow them all away.'

'That's good enough for me,' Drifter said. 'Gabe, Lefty, what do you think?'

'I say let's ride,' Gabe said impatiently. 'Our horses are fresh and if we push it, hopefully we can catch up with that crow-bait.'

'I second that,' Latigo said.

'Fair enough,' Drifter said. Then to Raven: 'One last question: can you tell by the prints if anyone is riding double?'

'Just one,' she replied. She pointed to another set of hoof prints. 'Look. See how much deeper they are? That means there's more weight on the horse.'

'Maybe it's a pack-mule,' Latigo said,

'or a spare horse carrying supplies?'

Raven shook her head. 'Then all the prints would be the same depth. These aren't. Only the back hoof prints are deeper. Which means the extra weight's on the horse's rump and — '

'It's most likely *El Espada*,' Drifter said. 'He's probably got Ingrid with him.'

'But there were three white women,' Liberty reminded. 'Why's she the only one riding double?'

'The other two are dead,' Gabe said. 'They got trampled to death when everyone tried to get out through the tunnel.'

'Christ, what a fiasco,' Liberty said quietly.

'Well, at least Ingrid's alive,' Drifter said. 'That's if it is her.'

'If it is,' said Liberty, 'the fact that *El Espada* has her with him is a good sign.'

'How you figure that?' Gabe said.

'It suggests he intends to take care of her.'

'So he can ransom her after he's

through with her?'

'Most likely, yes.'

'Who to?' Drifter said. 'Her husband's dead and her family is back in Norway.'

'*El Espada* probably doesn't know that,' Liberty said. 'He kidnapped her from her ranch near Santa Rosa. He probably assumes that she has relatives in town that would gladly pay him gold to get her back in one piece.'

Drifter wasted no more time. 'Mount up,' he told everyone. 'And let's push these horses until they drop.'

'What about him?' Liberty said, indicating Adelmo.

'Bring him along. Oh,' Drifter added, for Liberty's sake, 'to make sure he don't slow us down, let him double up with Raven. She's so light the horse will never know the difference.'

19

Following Adelmo's directions, they rode hard toward the mountains. It was not an easy ride; especially once the sun came up. A blazing white-gold orb, it shone right in their faces forcing them to pull down their hat-brims in order to protect their eyes from the intense glare.

The trail led them through narrow, steep-walled canyons and treacherous rock-strewn ravines, across open scrubland and dry riverbeds, where the dust kicked up by the horses' hooves stung their eyes and threatened to choke them.

Already hot, it got hotter as they reached the final five miles of flat open desert that stretched to the brown, rocky foothills below the mountains. Over the years it had become an indiscriminate graveyard for adventurous settlers, lost gold-miners and hungry prospectors and their bleached white bones lay scattered on both sides of the trail. Fortunately, Drifter had made sure everyone's canteens were full and an occasional sip of warm, metallic-tasting water moistened their parched throats and relieved their mounting thirst.

Every few miles they stopped to give the sweat-caked horses a blow. Each time they did Drifter had Raven examine the ground for the loose-shoe hoof print in order to make sure Adelmo was not leading them away from the hideout.

But it was always there and shortly after midday, they reached the barren foothills. Reining up in the shade of a rocky outcrop, Drifter asked Adelmo how close they were to the hideout.

'Don't lie to me, *amigo*,' he said as the Mexican refused to meet his gaze. 'I already warned you what would happen to you if you did.'

'No, lie, *señor*,' Adelmo said hastily. 'What I say before is truth.'

'Then look me in the eye, dammit.' When the Mexican wouldn't, Drifter turned to Gabe, saying: 'Something's gnawing at him. Before we go any farther and maybe walk into a trap, find out what it is.'

'Let me talk to him alone,' Gabe said. 'He might be more willing to open up.'

'Go ahead. But make it short.'

Gabe pulled Adelmo aside and spoke briefly with him, then returned to Drifter. 'It's his wife and young'uns.'

'What about them?'

'He says *El Espada* will torture them so that they die slowly and in great pain when he finds out Adelmo betrayed him.'

'Little late for regrets,' Drifter said coldly.

'But not too late to welcome a chance to find Ingrid.'

'Meaning?'

'He'll tell you what you want to know, but then you got to shoot him.'

''Mean . . . *kill* him?'

Gabe nodded.

Drifter frowned. He glanced at Adelmo, trying to figure the Mexican out and then turned back to Gabe, asking: 'You sure about that, *amigo*? I mean, could you have misunderstood him?'

'Nope. I asked him three times just to be certain.'

'That'd be mighty close to murder.'

Gabe shrugged. 'Or a mercy killing.'

Drifter exhaled loudly. 'Okay. It's his grave. But before I oblige him I got to be sure the hideout is where he says it is.'

'I already went over that with him. He'll take me there to prove he ain't lying. Then, when we get back, you have to shoot him.'

'Fair enough. Did he say how far away it was?'

'Not far — maybe thirty minutes.'

'Fine.' Drifter pulled out his Hamilton time piece. 'It's coming up on one o'clock. You got an hour to reach the hideout and get back here. If you don't show by then, tell him I'll comb these hills until I find it myself and then I'll spread the word that he told us where it was . . . which means God help his family.'

20

After Gabe and Adelmo had ridden off, Drifter stretched out beside Liberty, Raven and Latigo who, after hobbling the horses, were now resting in the shade.

Liberty seemed troubled by something and kept looking at her father, her big gold-brown eyes full of questions.

Finally Drifter said: 'You got something to say, daughter, speak your piece.'

Liberty hesitated, not sure how to approach the subject, and then said: 'I was wondering . . . do you intend to shoot Adelmo or are you running another bluff?'

'Depends on what Gabe has to say when they get back.'

'What if Morales is telling the truth and leads Gabe to the hideout? Will you oblige him with a bullet?'

'If he still wants me to, yes. It was his idea,' Drifter reminded her when her scowl suggested she found the idea distasteful. 'Says it's the only way to — '

'Save his family, yes, I heard. But that doesn't make it any less barbaric.'

'Jesus,' Drifter said. 'There's just no end to those bookwords, is there?'

Liberty ignored his sarcasm, said: 'There must be another way.'

'Find me one and I'll happily consider it. Unless, of course, you're going to pull rank on me again and decide for yourself?'

Liberty unpinned her badge and pocketed it. '*That* answer your question?'

Latigo, who'd been watching them as he rolled a smoke, chuckled softly then feigned innocence when Drifter glared at him. 'Don't mind me, Ace,' he said. 'I'm just sitting here filling a blanket.'

Though exasperated, Drifter held his temper and leaned against the rock to rest. The sun continued to beat down and even in the shade it grew unbearably hot.

'There's another way,' Raven said, finally breaking the silence.

'To do what,' Drifter replied, 'roll a smoke?'

'To not shoot *Señor* Morales.'

'I'm listening.'

'Shoot *El Espada* first.'

'First?'

'Before he can kill *Señor* Morales.'

Drifter smiled tolerantly. 'That would work,' he agreed. 'But we might have trouble convincing *El Espada* to cooperate.'

'He won't have a choice,' Raven said smugly. 'Not if I lead you to him.'

Drifter, for the first time, took her seriously. 'You can do that?'

'If you give me the chance, sure.'

Drifter looked at Liberty and Latigo, who both shrugged as if to say what have we got to lose?

'All right,' Drifter told Raven. 'Lead the way.'

'There's just one thing,' Latigo said as they all stood up. 'If we're going to do this, we got to reach the hideout before Gabe and Morales.'

'He's right,' Liberty agreed. 'Otherwise, if *El Espada* sees them first, he might make another run for it before we can put a bullet in him.'

Drifter looked at Raven. 'Can we do that?'

'Not if you all keep jawing,' she said.

Drifter hid a smile. 'You heard the lady. Saddle up.'

21

There were very few trees or bushes on the sunbaked hill, mostly rocks and sandy red dirt that made it easy for Raven to follow the hoof prints made by Gabe and Adelmo's horses.

There were other tracks present but Raven seemed to know which ones to follow and this time Latigo made no attempt to question her judgment. With Raven leading, the four of them kept their horses moving at a brisk trot and it wasn't long before they spotted Gabe and Adelmo riding slowly ahead of them.

Drifter reined up and motioned for the others to do the same, explaining: 'Until we can actually see the hideout, we can't risk Morales seeing us or it could sour our only chance of finding Ingrid.'

'That's assuming she's there,' Latigo said.

'Momma's there,' Raven said emphatically. 'She's got to be!'

They rode on, always hanging back enough so that they wouldn't be seen.

They hadn't long to wait. After ten minutes or so Gabe and Adelmo stopped at the entrance to a steep-walled canyon and dismounted.

Behind them, Drifter and the others did the same.

'I want you to stay here and take care of the horses,' Drifter told Raven. 'And this time,' he added, 'stay put — no matter how much shooting you hear. Got that?'

She scowled defiantly at him. 'What if you don't come back?'

'Don't worry. We will.'

Raven hesitated.

'I need your word on this,' Drifter insisted. 'I have to know you'll be here when we get back — you and the horses.'

Raven still didn't answer.

'Don't you want to stick around so you can see your mother when we get back with her?' Liberty said.

Swayed, Raven nodded. 'All right,' she told Drifter. 'I give you my word.' Collecting the four horses, she led them to a nearby patch of dried-out, leafless bushes that looked more dead than alive. Tying the reins to the branches she hunkered down in the sun-scorched dirt, rested her .22 rifle across her knees and sat there, motionless, like the Mescaleros had taught her.

Drifter, Liberty and Latigo took a moment to make sure their weapons were fully loaded before hurrying after Gabe and Adelmo, who were already scrambling up a steep rocky slope that climbed to the cliff-tops overlooking the canyon floor.

Latigo shaded his eyes against the sun and watched them for a moment. 'They must be part mountain goat,' he grumbled. He ducked as dirt and stones, kicked loose by Gabe and Adelmo's boots, showered over him. 'Part buffalo, too.'

'Will you quit bitching, Lefty,' Drifter said.

Latigo ignored him and fastidiously brushed the dirt from his clothes.

Drifter, Liberty and Latigo slowly made their way up the cliff-face. Now and then they had to ignore the falling dirt and rocks. They tried to avoid them but occasionally one bounced off their head, making them curse under their breath.

It was a steep grueling climb, made worse by the intense heat, and when they finally reached the top they collapsed, exhausted, behind some ancient black lava rocks that resembled pumice. It took a few moments to recover but once they did, they cautiously peered around the rocks . . .

What they saw surprised them: fifty yards ahead, across a rocky, black lava bed that wasn't visible from the canyon floor, stood a large volcanic mound that was honeycombed with caves. All of them appeared to be uninhabited, even the largest one, the entrance to which was among the rocks at the base of the mound.

As Drifter and the others watched, Adelmo led Gabe past the large cave and on up the slope to an opening between two rocks. Though it was narrow, Adelmo easily squeezed inside. Gabe followed, but being much bigger, got stuck halfway through. He struggled to get free, but couldn't and finally needed Adelmo's help to squeeze on through into the cave.

Drifter waited until Gabe disappeared, then he and the others ran to the foot of the mound below the opening. Here, Latigo refused to go any farther.

'But what if we need you once we get inside?' Liberty demanded.

'We won't,' Drifter said. He grabbed his daughter's arm and pulled her along after him, adding: 'You're wasting your breath. Lefty's afraid of tight places.'

'I heard that!' Latigo exclaimed. Then to Liberty: 'I ain't *afraid*. I just don't like being shut up in them is all.'

'Well, that's just great,' Liberty exclaimed as she and her father labored up the slope to the narrow opening. 'We're about to take on God knows how many Comancheros and our fastest gun has claustrophobia!'

22

Liberty had no difficulty squeezing through the opening. But Drifter, like Gabe, got stuck and needed his daughter to grab his arm and pull him on into the cave.

It was a small cave, no bigger than a tent, and the low ceiling forced Drifter and Liberty to hunch down in order not to hit their heads. There was no light other than the sunshine filtering in through the narrow entrance and they stood there for a few minutes, waiting for their eyes to get accustomed to the near-darkness.

'Where the hell did they go?' Drifter said, realizing the cave was empty.

'Through there, maybe.' Liberty pointed to a small natural opening at the rear. 'Looks like the entrance to another cave or maybe even a tunnel.'

'I'll be jiggered,' her father said. He

struck a match on his thumbnail, squinting as it flared and lit up the darkness.

'We're obviously not the first ones to use this cave,' Liberty said, indicating several half-burned pieces of wood lying scattered about them.

'No. But who were they? That's the question.'

Liberty shrugged. 'Hard to say. All that lava outside means this mound was once spewed up by a volcano. But that was millions of years ago — '

'These torches are recent,' Drifter said. 'Not prehistoric.'

'Which probably means they belonged to miners or prospectors?'

'Reckon that's as good a guess as any,' Drifter said. He picked up one of the torches, lit it and blew out the match.

'Here's another one,' Liberty said. 'They were all left here by people on their way out, which suggests there's no other exit.'

'Then where'd Gabe and Adelmo go?'

'Only one way to find out.'

'For true,' Drifter agreed. 'Follow me.' He led the way into the tunnel.

Hewn out of the rock by nature, the tunnel descended gradually for the first twenty paces but then as it continued to wind downward, the ground underfoot quickly steepened until they had to brace their outstretched hands against the walls in order not to slip and fall.

Presently Drifter stopped and held up his hand to Liberty. 'Am I loco,' he whispered, 'or do I hear voices?'

She listened and then nodded. 'Mexicans — lots of them.' She listened again before saying quietly: 'They're below us somewhere.'

'Wait here,' Drifter said. Handing her the fluttering torch, he cautiously inched downward. It was slow, treacherous going. Gradually, the light from the torch became fainter and fainter until he could barely see in front of him. After every few steps he stopped and listened and each time the voices grew louder.

They continued on. Then, unexpectedly, the tunnel ahead of him brightened. Puzzled, Drifter stopped and drew his Colt. Then pressing his left hand against the wall for support, he slowly descended toward the light.

A short distance ahead the tunnel leveled off and curved sharply to the left.

Drifter edged forward. When he reached the peak of the curve, he flattened himself against the volcanic rock and peered around the wall.

About twenty feet in front of him Gabe and Adelmo lay on their bellies at the edge of a large jagged hole in the ground. Necks craned, they were watching something going on below them. Firelight yellowed their faces while above them the ceiling of the cave had been blackened by centuries of smoke.

Drifter bent down, grasped a small stone and tossed it at Gabe. It bounced off his back causing him turn quickly, his right hand reaching for his six-gun.

He relaxed as he saw it was Drifter and whispered something to Adelmo. The Mexican turned his head, surprised to see Drifter, but said nothing.

Gabe signaled for Drifter to join them, at the same time motioning for him to get down on the ground. Drifter obeyed and crawled alongside Gabe. There, he peered over the edge of the hole.

Some fifty feet below was a cavern filled with Comancheros, all drinking tequila around a campfire. Most of them were drunk and fondling equally drunk women. All but two of the women were half-breeds or Comanche squaws. The remaining two were redheads, with sunburned white skin, and by their dull expressions and sluggish movements were either drunk or drugged, or both.

'What about the blond woman,' Drifter asked Gabe, 'have you seen her?'

'Yeah. When we first crawled out here she was over there with *El Espada*.'

Gabe pointed to the right side of the fire. 'Son of a bitch had a rope around her neck, like she was some kind of goddamn dog!'

Drifter cursed inwardly. 'Was it Ingrid?'

Gabe nodded glumly.

'You sure?'

'Positive. I got a good look at her face.'

'Where are they now — do you know?'

'He dragged her into that tunnel.' Gabe indicated a narrow opening next to a much larger one. 'There's a cave in there. You can't see it from here, but Adelmo says that *El Espada* only uses it when he has a woman.'

'What about the big tunnel?'

'It leads to another cave where — '

' — they keep their horses?'

'Yeah. How'd you — ?'

'The droppings.' Drifter indicated a trail of dung leading into the tunnel. He then thumbed at a huge round boulder blocking the entrance to a tunnel opposite them. 'Is that how they get in and out?'

Gabe nodded.

'Where's the outside entrance?'

'Between two big fist-shaped rocks about halfway into the canyon.'

'North or south wall?'

'South. You can see it easily enough, but you can't get near it. Not without being seen.'

'Lookouts?'

'On top of the cliffs on both sides of the canyon . . . with orders to shoot anyone they see nosing around.'

Drifter considered Gabe's warning before saying: 'Suppose I somehow managed to sneak past the lookouts into the tunnel, how do these butchers roll that big boulder aside when they want to leave?'

''Cording to Adelmo, they wedge those poles' — he indicated a pile of spruce poles near the boulder — 'under it.'

'That can't be easy — 'specially if they got smoke in their eyes.'

'Smoke?'

Drifter thumbed at an ancient rock-fall behind them. 'If you throw some of those rocks down into the fire, the result's going to be like dynamite — flames and hot coals flying everywhere, forcing those bastards to scatter like scalded cats.'

'Then I pick them off, one by one?'

'That's the plan. But don't shoot any of the fellas rolling that rock aside — least not until they're finished. Otherwise, we won't be able to get in.'

Gabe frowned. 'Let me get this straight, *compadre*. I toss a few rocks in the fire, causing a lot of smoke that hopefully forces those bastards to panic and roll that big rock aside so they can get out, while you — '

'And Emily — '

'Emily's with you?'

'Yeah, she's waiting back up the tunnel. Anyway,' Drifter added, 'all you got to do is give us enough time to get down to the canyon and into the

141

tunnel, then start throwing. That way, she and I — and Latigo, too, if he hasn't gotten bored and decided to ride off — will be there to shoot the Comancheros when they roll the rock aside. Then, if our luck's holding, we'll find *El Espada*, gun him down and get Ingrid the hell out of there.'

Gabe almost laughed. The plan was so full of 'ifs' he knew it was destined to fail that he couldn't find words to express himself.

Adelmo spoke for him. '*Usted necesita un milagro, señor.*'

Drifter frowned. 'What'd he say?'

'That you need a miracle.'

'Only one? How 'bout six or seven?'

Gabe wasn't amused. He sighed, heavy-hearted, and offered Drifter his hand. 'Good luck, *compadre*. See you soon.'

Drifter could tell Gabe didn't expect him to make it. But he'd beaten the odds before, so why not now? Forcing himself to sound optimistic, he said: 'That will be thirty minutes from now, when I come out of that tunnel, guns a-blazing.'

''*Guns a-blazing?*''

'Guns a-blazing.'

Gabe rolled his eyes. 'And you got the gall to accuse *me* of reading too many goddamned dime novels!'

23

Gabe and Adelmo once more lay on their bellies, only now between them was a pile of rocks that they had rolled to the edge of the hole. Gabe checked his pocket-watch and held up five fingers the nervous, sweating Mexican. Adelmo nodded to show that he understood and went on anxiously chewing his lip.

It wasn't a good sign and Gabe, worried that in the remaining five minutes Adelmo might panic and run off, assured him that everything was going to be fine.

'You are sure of this?' Adelmo asked him in Spanish.

'Sure as I can be about anything,' Gabe replied. Then as a thought struck him: 'You got any family or relatives down there?'

'*Nada, señor.*'

'What if I gave you my rifle, would you help me shoot those fellas? It would be for your own good,' Gabe added, still speaking Spanish. 'If all the Comancheros are dead, then they can't torture or kill your family.'

'You would do this?' Adelmo said. 'You would trust me with your rifle?'

Gabe nodded. 'Just remember, *compadre*. You give me any reason to and I'll shoot you faster than you can spit. *Comprende?*'

'*Si, señor.*'

Gabe handed Adelmo his rifle and looked at his watch as the tiny second-hand ticked off the final minute. Then it came down to seconds. '. . . five, four, three, two, one. Ready?' he said, getting to his knees and grabbing a rock. '*Ahora!*'

He heaved the rock over the edge and watched it drop into the center of the blazing fire. Beside him, Adelmo did the same.

The impact of the rocks scattered the fire, sending flames, sparks and burning logs flying everywhere. Panicked, the Comancheros pushed their women aside and scrambled away from the fire.

By then Gabe and Adelmo had dropped two more rocks into the dying flames. The first one smashed into the glowing embers, hurling them about the cavern, while the second hit a big cauldron of beans hanging from a spit over the fire. The cauldron overturned. The hot coals hissed as beans and juice splashed over them, dousing the flames and filling the cavern with smoke.

Alarmed, the Comancheros and their women staggered blindly about, pawing at their eyes. The few bandits who could still see grabbed the spruce poles and ran to the boulder blocking the tunnel entrance. There, they started prying the boulder aside, shouting at each other to hurry!

Gabe and Adelmo started shooting the Comancheros who weren't working on the boulder. The gunfire and cries from the dying and wounded brought

El Espada running out of the smaller tunnel.

Gabe shot at him. But smoke was now rising through the hole, making his eyes water, and he missed. The bullet ricocheted off the rock wall near *El Espada's* head, warning him that he was being targeted, and he ran back into the tunnel.

When he reappeared moments later, he held Ingrid in front of him like a shield. He had a six-gun in his free hand and as he looked upward, eyes also watering from the smoke, he glimpsed Gabe firing over the edge of the hole. He snapped off two shots, the bullets close enough to force Gabe to jump back.

Adelmo wasn't as lucky. *El Espada's* third shot punched a hole in the Mexican's forehead, killing him instantly. Legs buckling, he pitched forward, down through the hole, and landed in the middle of the dying fire.

Enraged, Gabe grabbed up his rifle and returned to the edge of the hole.

The swirling smoke hid almost everyone below, including *El Espada* and Ingrid, but whenever a Comanchero stumbled into view Gabe shot him. It was easier than shooting wooden ducks at a country fair. The hapless Comancheros didn't try to fight back; as one, they crowded about the tunnel entrance, where their brethren were desperately trying to roll the boulder aside.

Above them, Gabe moved around the edge of the hole until he was directly opposite the boulder. There, he began picking off the Comancheros who weren't handling the spruce poles. Their dying cries added to panic and chaos.

Finally, the bandits managed to move the boulder away from the entrance to the tunnel. Everyone surged forward, fighting each other to escape Gabe's bullets.

But they were crammed so tightly together, their bodies blocked the entrance. They became wedged there, all of them yelling and wildly punching at one another.

Gabe stopped shooting, sickened by the sight of the crumpled bodies of the two redheads. Neither of the women showed any signs of life and he grimly realized that they had been trampled to death by the panicked Comancheros.

It didn't seem like it could get any worse.

It was then Drifter and Liberty, who had worked their way along the tunnel and now stood facing the trapped Comancheros, opened fire.

There was no way they could miss their targets. The front row of bandits died where they stood, while those directly behind them tripped over the corpses and went sprawling.

Drifter and Liberty emptied their guns into them before they could get up, killing them where they lay. It didn't stop there. The Comancheros behind them stumbled helplessly over the rows of corpses and were also shot, causing a domino effect that soon turned into a mass grave.

Overhead, Gabe continued to pick off the Comancheros that were at the back of the crowd. They too died where they stood. It didn't take long for the others to realize they were again caught in a withering crossfire. Trapped in the dark, narrow confines of the tunnel, the sight of their dead and dying comrades soon forced the remaining Comancheros to drop their guns and raise their hands in surrender.

Drifter and Liberty approached them cautiously, ready to shoot anyone who made an aggressive move. But the cowed bandits made no attempt to jump them or to pick up their weapons and Drifter and Liberty quickly kicked them out of reach.

'Keep these hog-lickers covered,' Drifter told her, 'while I go hunt down *El Espada* and Ingrid.'

'I've got a better idea,' she replied. '*You* keep them covered while I go after *El Espada*.'

'Thought you weren't going to pull rank?'

'I'm not. I'm just doing my job as a lawman.'

Drifter gave her a sour look. 'One day, *Marshal*, that tin star of yours is going to buy you a pine box.'

'I knew that, Daddy, when I took the oath.' Liberty studied her father for a beat, her expression a strange mix of defiance and tolerance, then, softening, said: 'I know it's hard for you to think of me as anything but your little girl, but you have to try. I'm all grown up now and I need to stand on my own two feet.'

Drifter sighed, and grudgingly held back his feelings.

'He's just trying to save your life,' a voice said in the darkness behind Liberty.

She whirled around and saw Gabe standing behind her.

'You stay out of this, Mr. Moonlight. This is between Daddy and me.'

'Reckon any father would do the

same in his place.'

'Only if they didn't think I was capable of taking *El Espada*.'

'That's not true,' Drifter said. 'I'm sure you are. It's just, why take that chance when I'm willing to take it for you?'

'Because it's my job. And if I don't at least try, I'll never have any confidence. Worse, I'll never respect myself or become the Marshal I expect to be.'

Drifter shrugged and expelled his frustration in a long sigh.

'Okay,' he said. 'If it means that much to you, I reckon I can't stand in your way — ' He stopped as shots were heard outside in the canyon.

'Latigo!' Gabe exclaimed. 'I told him to start shooting if he saw either Ingrid or *El Espada*!'

24

When Drifter, Liberty and Gabe burst out of the entrance to the cavern, there was no sign of Latigo — or Raven.

'Dammit,' Drifter said, blinking in the sunlight. 'She gave me her word she'd stay put.'

'Then someone forced her to move,' Gabe said, ''cause Raven never breaks her word, no matter what.'

'Always a first time,' Drifter grumbled.

'Maybe,' Gabe said, looking off at something. 'But this ain't it.' He thumbed toward Raven, who emerged from a nearby gully, leading their horses.

'Sorry I couldn't be here,' she said, stopping beside Drifter. 'But Mr. Rawlins and me, we saw *El Espada* leading my mother and Brandy out of that cave' — she pointed at the canyon entrance to the cavern — 'and I took a shot at him.'

'Did you hit him?'

'No. But I hit his horse. It went down and him with it. I was going to fire again, but I was afraid of hitting Momma.'

'What about Latigo?' Liberty demanded. 'What happened to him?'

'He's behind those rocks,' Raven said, pointing.

'Dead?'

'Uh-uh. Unconscious.'

''Mean he's been shot?'

She nodded. 'One of *El Espada's* bullets grazed him here' — she touched her left temple — 'and he went down. I thought at first he was dead but — '

Drifter cut her off. 'Then what happened?'

'*El Espada*, he ducked behind Momma's horse and started shooting at me.'

'Did your ma try to get away?' Gabe asked.

'She couldn't. Her hands were tied to

154

the saddle horn, and he had hold of the reins.'

'Go on,' Drifter urged when Raven paused. 'What happened next?'

'Well, we kept on shooting at each other and then Momma must've seen me or something, 'cause she hollered out my name, which wasn't too smart, 'cause then *El Espada*, he knew who I was and threatened to shoot Momma if I didn't throw out my gun.'

'Hell, you didn't fall for that old trick, did you?' Gabe demanded.

'Easy, *amigo*,' Drifter said. 'Let her finish, okay? Go on,' he told Raven. 'Then, what?'

'I broke off a branch from this ocotillo bush I was hiding behind and threw it out where he could see it, hoping he'd think it was my rifle. But he was too smart for that. He said I had five seconds to throw down my gun or he'd kill Momma. I knew I had to obey him. But before I could, she said something to him that made him change his mind. I don't know what it was, but next thing, Momma called out to me, saying I had to stop shooting and let them get away. I didn't want to but I did. *El Espada* then mounted Brandy and rode off with my mother. I thought about following them, but then I remembered I gave you' — she looked at Drifter — 'my word I'd stay put, so I did. But now that you're here, I'm going after her.'

'I wouldn't blame you if you did, Raven. But if you truly want to help your mother, you'd be better off staying here and helping Marshal Mercer.'

'Do what?'

'Stop the Comancheros from following us.'

Raven frowned, puzzled. 'How am I supposed to do that? I'm just a kid.'

Liberty said: 'Between the two of us, we can keep the Comancheros inside the cave until Drifter and Gabe get back.'

Raven eyed Liberty and the two men, uncertain. Then she said: 'What if you can't find *El Espada* or Momma?'

'We will,' Gabe promised. 'What's more, we'll bring her back, safe and sound. And that's the Bible truth!'

'All we're asking for,' Drifter said when Raven didn't answer, 'is that you give us the chance to try.'

Raven thought long and hard before saying: 'All right. I'll help the Marshal. But I warn you,' she threatened, 'if you don't find Momma and bring her back, then I'm going to spend the rest of my life tracking her down. And nothing you can say is going to make me change my mind.'

'We wouldn't even try,' Gabe assured her. 'Not for a moment.'

'That's for true,' Drifter agreed. 'It'd be your right.' To Gabe, he said: 'C'mon, let's find out how bad Lefty's hurt.'

25

They found the little Texas bounty hunter slumped down behind the rocks, holding a blood-stained kerchief to his temple. He'd just regained consciousness and was still groggy, prompting Drifter to ask him if he felt strong enough to ride.

'*El Espada*'s got Ingrid,' Gabe added, 'and we're going after them.'

'Count me in,' Latigo insisted. 'I got a bullet with that skunk's name on it.'

'I'll get the horses.' Gabe hurried off, leaving Drifter to help Latigo to his feet.

'Sure you're up to it?' Drifter asked as the gunman stood there, swaying unsteadily. ''Cause if you're not, say so. You'll only slow us down.'

'If you're trying to prod me, Ace, it ain't necessary. I'll ride to hell to kill that bastard. So you worry about your ulcers and let me worry about my head.'

'Fair enough,' Drifter said. 'Let's make tracks.'

His words were hidden by a sudden, loud explosion behind them. Startled, they whirled around just as a rockslide came thundering down the cliff-slope into the canyon. When the dust finally settled they saw that a huge pile of rocks now covered the entrance to the cavern.

Drifter slumped, as if punched. '*Madre de Dios!*'

'What's wrong?'

'Emily!'

'What about her?'

'She and Liberty are trapped in the cave!'

'Were,' Latigo corrected. He thumbed toward the base of the opposite cliff-face, where Liberty, Raven and Gabe now climbed out of a dry riverbed. 'Reckon they made it out just in time.'

Drifter sagged with relief. He and

Latigo hurried to the trio.

'Y-You okay?' Drifter asked Liberty.

'Sure.'

'Good. I was . . . was . . . '

'Worried about me?' Liberty said as his voice trailed off.

He shrugged in a way that could have meant anything.

'Is that a yes?'

'Maybe just a tad.'

'Careful, Daddy. Your emotions are showing.'

He knew she was needling him and managed a tight little smile. 'What the hell happened anyway? The explosion, I mean . . . what caused it?'

'One of the Comancheros had a stick of dynamite hidden under his shirt,' Raven said. 'He lit it and threw it at the Marshal — '

'Behind me,' Liberty corrected. 'Little cockroach didn't think I saw it, but I did and kicked it back at him. He tried to run away, but I shot him before he could and then got the hell out of there.'

160

'What about the other Comancheros?'

'Don't waste any tears on them. They must know another way out or else why would they risk being buried alive?'

It made sense and Drifter nodded.

Gabe said: 'We're losing valuable time here, Quint. Let's get to riding.'

Fortunately, Liberty and Raven had seen *El Espada* and Ingrid ride off, so they knew which direction he was headed. It also helped that the valleys, canyons and hillsides were badly parched, allowing Raven's keen eyesight to quickly find the two sets of different hoof prints in the dirt. One set showed four crisp imprints and belonged to a long-striding horse that Gabe insisted was Brandy; the other set was inconsistent: three of the prints were clean, while the fourth was messy and looked familiar. Once Raven spotted it, she whooped for joy and told Drifter: 'It's the same horse, the one Momma's riding.'

'Which same horse is that?'

'The one with the loose shoe of course! Goddlelmighty, now I can follow them anywhere!'

She was as good as her word. Riding alongside Drifter, she never lost sight of the two sets of hoof prints as they headed deep into the hot, barren foothills.

Though ever-watchful, none of them caught a glimpse of Ingrid or *El Espada*. And after they'd followed the meandering tracks for an hour or so, they reined up to give the horses a blow and to gulp thirstily from their canteens.

'Wonder where the hell the son of a bitch is headed?' Gabe said, frustrated.

'Wherever it is, Latigo grumbled, 'he keeps changing directions.'

'Most likely trying to cover his tracks,' Liberty said.

'Which could mean he knows we're following him,' Drifter added.

'Us — or someone,' said Latigo. 'For all we know there could be others dogging his trail.'

'Like who?' put in Liberty.

'I don't know. *Federales . . . rurales . . .* maybe even some of his own men.'

'Why would they pursue him?'

'Could be, they want Ingrid for themselves. Wouldn't be the first time a good-looking woman made men turn on each other.'

'Maybe if you had stronger convictions, we wouldn't be able to,' Liberty said.

Before Gabe could reply, Drifter said: 'Could also be a posse.'

'How you figure that?'

'Maybe someone in Santa Rosa told the Sheriff Ingrid's missing.'

'It's possible,' Gabe admitted.

'It's also possible that he's trying to double back on us,' Latigo said.

'Is he?' Drifter asked Raven.

She shook her head. 'Not unless he and Momma switched horses without dismounting somewhere. And that ain't likely.'

'What makes you so sure?' Latigo demanded.

''Cause if they changed horses, there'd be a whole bunch of jumbled-up hoof prints — and there ain't. 'Least, I haven't seen any.'

'Even so, that doesn't mean they don't exist,' Drifter said. 'And though I normally wouldn't press it, these aren't normal circumstances. Your ma's life is at stake and we can't afford to ignore any possibility, no matter how unlikely it is.'

'I agree,' Liberty said. '*El Espada* could have stashed fresh horses around here somewhere prior to today.'

'That would mean the bastard planned on coming here all along,' Gabe said.

'Exactly.'

'There's another unpleasant possibility to consider,' Latigo said grimly. 'He could've already doubled back and somehow gotten past us. All bunched up like we were, it wouldn't've been that hard.'

It was a sobering thought and for a moment it quieted everybody. Then:

'It's your call,' Drifter told Liberty. 'You want to go on or head back?'

'I think we should go on. But I also think we should spread out. That way it would be harder for them to get by us, should they actually try.'

'Makes sense,' Gabe agreed. 'How far apart do you want us, Marshal?'

'Depends on the terrain,' Liberty said. 'But always stay close enough so you can signal one another.'

'Who's going to stay with Raven?' Drifter asked.

'Would you?'

'Sure.'

'Okay then,' Liberty said. 'Let's fan out. And stay alert. *El Espada* probably knows this territory better than we do, so keep your eyes peeled.'

'What about my eyes?' Raven demanded indignantly. 'Did I suddenly go blind or something?'

'Your eyes will be busy looking for hoof prints,' Drifter reminded. 'That's your specialty.'

'Without you,' Gabe assured her,

'hell, we wouldn't know which way to go.'

'Truth is,' Liberty added, 'we wouldn't have even gotten this far.'

Latigo, irked by the attention Raven was getting, said irritably: 'If you three glad-handers are all through dishing out compliments, can we get moving? We're burning daylight. That's unless, of course, you don't care 'bout finding your ma anymore,' he said to Raven.

'I care,' she said defiantly. 'I care more than you've ever cared about anyone, so there.' Angrily fixing her eyes on the trail, she urged her horse forward.

'Dammit, quit riding her,' Drifter told Latigo. 'She's just a young'un and she's already got more grief than she needs.' Kicking his horse up, he rode after Raven.

Liberty looked disgustedly at Latigo. 'You just can't stop stirring the pot, can you, Mr. Rawlins?'

He whitened angrily but didn't say anything.

Liberty wheeled her horse around and reined up beside Gabe. They waited for Latigo, who grudgingly joined them. The three of them then fanned out until they were roughly a hundred yards apart and rode in a broken line that paralleled Drifter and Raven.

26

By now, Ingrid had given up all hope of being rescued. Hands roped to the saddle horn, she rode silently beside *El Espada* along a winding dirt trail that climbed to a rocky pass separating the foothills from the mountains.

She wondered how and when she was going to die. The uncertainty was driving her crazy. How she'd handled her life didn't make her feel any better. First, she'd been at least partly responsible for her husband's death, leaving her daughter fatherless, and now, through no fault of her own, her fate was in the hands of a ruthless killer. She wanted to scream, 'Why me?' but controlled herself. If there was a God, like she believed, she didn't feel that anyone had the right to blame all their troubles on a deity that had already given His children the greatest gift off all: life!

It was beyond comprehension. And though she hated the thought of dying and leaving Raven alone in the world, she prayed that death would come soon so she wouldn't have to suffer the mental agony that was far worse than any physical torture that *El Espada* could inflict on her.

They rode on in grim silence. Every now and then the Comanchero leader looked at her, a sidelong glance that was full of anger and contempt.

Finally it got too much for Ingrid. 'What do you intend to do with me?' she demanded. 'Sell me?'

He gave her a withering, scornful look, as if she wasn't worth answering.

'If you hate me so much and don't intend to sell me, why don't you let me go? I swear I won't say anything to the Sheriff or the Marshal.'

He laughed contemptuously. '*Usted es un gringo, señora.*'

'Speak English,' she told him. 'I know

you can. I heard you talking to one of your men.'

'You are a *gringo, señora,* and I no trust *gringos.* As for what I do with you,' he continued, 'I keep you till I tire of you. Then I sell to Comanches.'

The thought terrified her. But trying to remain calm, she said: 'Indians don't have any money. You'd be much better off selling me to a rich *hacendado.* I've heard Mexican ranchers will pay a lot for an American woman.'

El Espado smiled — a cruel thin-lipped smile that made Ingrid shiver.

'This is true, *señora.* But not after they have been soiled by Comancheros. Such a woman, even a *gringo,* is worth less than the lowest whore in Palomas.'

Though stung by his insult, Ingrid refused to show it and rode on in grim silence.

Ahead, the canyon quickly narrowed and the cliffs flanking them grew more and more sheer. They also gradually closed in on both sides. To Ingrid it seemed that they were running out of room. Soon, she realized, there would not be enough space for them to even squeeze through, let alone ride through on horseback.

Then as they rode around a rocky outcrop, an opening appeared in the cliffs. Big enough for them to enter on foot, it looked harmless enough. But as they reined up in front of it *El Espada* held his finger to his lips, warning her to be quiet.

Ingrid nodded to show she understood. Dismounting from her buckskin, she waited until the bandit had led his horse into the cave and then followed him.

The stench of bat *guano* was nauseating. But somehow she fought down the urge to vomit and led her horse onward. She had expected it to be dark, but not so dark that even when her eyes had grown accustomed to the darkness, she could barely see the rear of *El Espada*'s horse in front of her.

'I can't see,' she whispered after she'd

almost fallen. 'Can't you light a match or something?'

'*Silencio!*' *El Espada* hissed angrily.

Ingrid fell silent. But as she stumbled along, trying not to trip, the only way she could keep her balance was by pressing her hand on the wall beside her.

They had covered a short distance, the only light coming from the tiny sparks flying up each time the horses' hooves struck the stony ground, when suddenly something small and furry and clammy flew into Ingrid's face.

She gasped and tried to brush it away. But its claws had become entangled in her hair and, squeaking, it frantically fluttered its wings in an effort to break free. She again tried to knock it away. This time the bat bit her, its sharp teeth puncturing her hand, making her cry out.

El Espada hissed at her to be quiet, but it was too late.

Suddenly the darkness resonated with the fluttering of thousands of bats that dropped from the ceiling where they had been roosting after a night of gorging on insects. Awakened by Ingrid's startled cry, the squeaking, flying horde swept through the cave, terrifying the horses. They reared up, snorting with fear, jerking the reins out of Ingrid and *El Espada*'s hands and charging off into the darkness.

Slammed against the wall by her panicked buckskin, Ingrid lay on the ground, stunned, while squeaking bats swarmed all around her. It was like some hellish nightmare and after everything else she'd already endured it was too much for her mind to conquer. Overwhelmed, she felt herself growing dizzy and faint . . . the thunderous fluttering all around her slowly fading until it seemed to be coming from far off . . . followed by a darkness even darker than the cave that swept over her until everything became quiet; still; peaceful.

27

Drifter saw it first. Thinking it was smoke spiraling up from the cliffs ahead, he pointed it out to the others, saying: 'Reckon we've finally found their hideout.'

'Thank God,' Liberty groaned. She looked at Gabe and Raven and they all sighed gratefully.

But Latigo, whose sight was keenest, shook his head. 'It ain't smoke, it's bats.'

'Bats?' Raven questioned.

He nodded. 'I seen it once before. 'Cross the border in Arizona. They're flying out of their cave, thousands and thousands of them. 'Cept this time it's different.'

'How?' said Drifter.

'This is daytime. And bats only hunt after sundown, when it's getting dark.'

Gabe frowned at him. 'Is this another

one of your campfire jokes?'

'No joke,' Latigo said. 'I talked to this old silver miner once. Said bats don't need light to see, and they know it's safer outside for them to hunt when it's dark.'

Drifter, who'd been watching the bats flooding into the gold-blue sky, said: 'Something must've frightened them.'

'Or some*one*,' Latigo said darkly.

'Like, *El Espada*?' Liberty suggested.

'Could be.'

'Wait a minute,' Gabe said. 'You saying this cave the bats are flying out of, is the Comancheros' hideout?'

'More likely the entrance to it,' Drifter said. 'Right, Lefty?'

'That'd be my guess, Ace.'

'Mine too,' Drifter said. 'Mount up, everybody. We'll go take a closer look.'

When they reached the narrow end of the canyon, there were still a few bats flying in and out of the cave. The others were darting back and forth overhead. Dismounting, Drifter and the others were about to lead their horses inside when Raven suddenly pointed at something in the dirt.

'Look!' she exclaimed. 'It's the same print.' She knelt down, pointing. 'See! It's not in — in — ' She paused and looked at Liberty for help.

'Intact?'

'Right. Not intact like them other three prints. This one's half-filled with dirt.'

'Caused by that loose shoe?'

Raven nodded. 'See for yourself.'

Liberty knelt beside her and examined the hoof print. 'You're right, missy.' Then straightening up, she thumbed at the cave and said to Drifter: 'The two of them went in there. I'd bet the bank on it.'

Latigo nervously licked his lips. 'Does that mean we're going in after 'em?'

Before Drifter could answer, a bat swooped down and flew, squeaking, over his head. He ducked, more amused than alarmed, and the low-flying bat darted away. Liberty was in its path. Panicking, she gasped and fearfully covered her head with her hands. The bat narrowly missed her and streaked upward, rejoining the other bats circling in the sky.

'Quick,' she said to Gabe. 'Help me find something that'll burn.'

He chuckled. 'Frightened of bats, are you, Marshal?'

'Petrified,' she admitted. 'I get nightmares just thinking about them.'

'In that case,' Drifter said, 'why don't you wait here while we look around?'

'No, thanks,' Liberty said, 'I'll take my chances with the rest of you.'

28

Before entering the cave, they ripped up one of Gabe's old shirts and tied the pieces around the hooves of their horses to muffle any sound. Drifter then took the almost empty bottle of whiskey from his saddlebags and insisted each person dab some of it under their nose. He then swigged the last drop, tossed the bottle away and led them into the cave. The smell of the whiskey tempered the stench of the bat *guano*, but the sickening odor still made them gag.

Led by Drifter, they moved across the cave and into the tunnel beyond. The light from Liberty's flaming torch showed the ground and walls were covered in bat droppings. It also showed the two sets of footprints and hoof prints made by Ingrid and *El Espada* and their horses, the outlines visible in the inches-deep bat *guano*.

As Liberty led her horse along, she anxiously glanced about her. But there were no longer any bats in the cave or in the long winding tunnel that nature had carved through the foothills, and gradually she lost her fear of being attacked.

After ten minutes or so, the tunnel became lighter. They could now dimly see about them. A short distance ahead was a severe right-angled bend. Unable to see what was beyond it, Drifter signaled to the others to stop. He then gave the reins to Gabe to hold and cautiously started around the bend. He was only gone for a few minutes, but when he reappeared he looked excited.

'There's an opening just ahead,' he explained. 'It leads out into a box-canyon that's being used for a hideout.'

'What about Ingrid and *El Espada*?' Gabe said. 'Did you see them?'

'Uh-uh. But there's a shed by an old played-out mine and a bunch of cabins built back among some trees. Most likely they're in one of them.'

'How many lookouts they got posted?' Latigo said.

'That's the rub,' Drifter replied. 'I didn't see a single one.'

'They must feel pretty safe in there,' Liberty said.

'Either that,' Gabe said, 'or they're so well hid you can't see 'em.'

'Could be,' Drifter admitted. 'But there were men and women gathered outside what looked like a general store, and I saw children playing by the cabins, so I'd say Liberty's right.'

Liberty cocked an eyebrow at her father. 'Do you know that that's the first time you've ever called me Liberty?'

Drifter frowned, as if not sure how to reply, then said: 'Been a long day.'

'If that's an excuse, Daddy, you don't need one. I like both names. It was just — well, a surprise is all.'

'These people you saw?' Raven said to Drifter. 'Were they Comancheros?'

'Hold your tongue, young'un,' Latigo snapped, 'else I'll cut it off.'

'Quit picking on her,' Drifter said. 'She's got a right to know, same as the rest of us. 'Sides, it's a fair question and deserves a fair answer. I didn't count heads,' he said to Raven. 'But from what I saw, most of them are. On top of that, there's livestock penned up in the corrals, most of 'em with different brands — '

'Any of the cattle carrying Ingrid's brand?' Gabe asked.

'I couldn't tell. They were all milling around. I also saw smoke coming from all the cabins, which means folks are living in them.'

'You think they're outlaws?' Liberty asked.

'Be no reason to live there if they weren't,' put in Latigo.

'He's right,' said Gabe. 'Place like this, hell, it's probably just like the Hole in the Wall. Bunch of different gangs, with different leaders, who don't tread on each other's toes and figure there's safety in numbers.'

Surprised, Raven asked Gabe: 'When

were you in Montana?'

'Never,' he replied. 'But back in '84 I was in Wyoming for a spell and I ran into Kid Curry. He was hiding out at the Hole with the rest of the Cassidy gang and invited me to join them.'

'Did you?' Drifter asked.

'Hell, no. I may have robbed a bank or two and even a few trains since I crossed the border, but that don't mean I'm anything like the rustlers, renegades and misfits holed up in that rat's nest. They'd slit your throat for a bent *centavo*. 'Sides,' he added to Raven, 'I love you and your mom too much to run out on you.'

'If you love us so much,' she scoffed, 'how come you never mentioned going to the Hole in the Wall?'

Gabe shrugged. 'Didn't figure it was important. Thanks to the *federales* always dogging my trail I don't see you two as much as I'd like, so when I do manage to shake the law long enough to sneak across the border, I got far better things to discuss than joining up with the likes of Kid Curry or Butch Cassidy.'

'I suppose so,' Raven said.

Drifter turned to Liberty. 'We're wasting precious time here. Tell us what you want to do about Ingrid?'

'We came here to rescue her,' she said firmly, 'and that's what I intend to do.'

'Count me in,' Gabe said.

'Me, too,' said Latigo.

'Goes without saying,' Drifter added.

'Okay then,' Liberty said. 'Let's get this done.'

The four of them made sure their weapons were fully loaded and then Drifter led them along the tunnel to the natural opening in the hillside. Here, they removed the padding from the hooves of their horses before stepping up into the saddle.

'I'll take over from here,' Liberty told Drifter.

'Help yourself.'

'The way I see it,' she said, addressing everyone, 'we've got two ways to play this. We wait till dark and hope to catch them by surprise — which, since we don't know where they're holding Mrs. Bjorkman, may not be possible — or, go in now, when everyone can see us, and act like we have every right to be there.'

'In other words,' Drifter said, 'pretend we're outlaws?'

Liberty nodded. 'Other than *El Espada*, there's a good chance no one else would know who we are — especially since Gabe, here, is a known outlaw anyway.'

'It might work,' Gabe said, 'so long as no one recognizes Lefty.'

'Why should they?' Latigo said. 'It's been a spell since I crossed the border to hunt down a fugitive.'

'Good,' Liberty said. 'Then I say we go in now and try to find Mrs. Bjorkman.' She turned to Latigo, adding: 'You bring up the rear. And you,' she said to Gabe, 'take the lead. We'll follow you as if we're all part of your gang. Oh, and Raven, if there's any shooting, take cover and stay there until it's over. Understood?'

Raven scowled, displeased, but reluctantly nodded.

'All right, gentlemen,' Liberty said, 'let's go find Mrs. Bjorkman.' She eased her horse past Drifter and rode through the opening out into the open.

29

With Gabe leading the way, the five of them rode down the steep rocky hillside, following the narrow winding trail that descended to the valley floor. When they reached the bottom, the land was flat and save for a few scattered rocks there was no cover to hide them from the men and women gathered outside the general store or from the families who were busy working around their cabins. They rode in a tightly bunched group, Gabe slightly ahead, everyone sitting tall and relaxed in the saddle as if they had every right to be there.

The ploy worked. Except for a few curious looks, no one paid much attention to them and they reached the small, log-walled general store unchallenged. Here, they dismounted and tied their horses to the rail by the entrance.

'You two stay with the horses,' Liberty told Latigo and Raven. 'And if anyone starts acting suspiciously, let me know.'

'Maybe I should go in with you,' Latigo said. 'Could be there's more guns in there than you can handle.'

'If there are, and you hear shooting, you're welcome to join the party,' she said with a slight smile. She then led Drifter and Gabe into the store.

Latigo looked at Raven, who was busy tightening the straps of her saddlebags. 'Wouldn't be the first time I've had to wet-nurse your pa and Gabe,' he said.

If Raven was impressed, she didn't show it. Satisfied that the straps were properly fastened, she turned and watched as Latigo rolled a cigarette.

'You smoke?' he asked her.

'Not yet.'

'Don't know what you're missing.'

'Says you,' she said defiantly.

'Don't sass me, girl.'

'Didn't think I was.'

Latigo let that slide. Licking the edge of the paper, he sealed the cigarette and wetted the end before putting it between his lips. He then flared a match, cupped his hands around the flame and lit up. His cheeks caved in as he inhaled deeply and then billowed as he expelled a lungful of smoke. 'Mm-mmm,' he sighed. 'Nothing like the taste of tobacco.'

Raven, who'd been eyeing Latigo's guns, said: 'If I ask you a question, Mr. Rawlins, do you promise not say I'm sassing you?'

'Depends on the question.'

'Do you think folks respect you for being the fastest gun around?'

''Course.'

'That's not what Momma says. She says it's 'cause they're scared of you.'

'Same thing, ain't it?'

Raven chewed on that before playing her ace. 'Know what else Momma said?'

'Tell me.'

'That the day's coming when men won't have to carry guns and then gunmen like you won't be needed no more. You'll be' — she paused, trying to remember the word her mother used — 'extinct, like them big giant creatures that used to roam the earth millions of years ago.'

'You mean dinosaurs?'

'Yeah, that's the word: dinosaurs.'

Latigo laughed. 'Shows you how much your ma knows, girl. Men will always need guns. How else we supposed to protect ourselves and our womenfolk?'

'Same way they do back east. Pay the police to do it for you. Did you know,' she continued, 'that in most cities nowadays it's against the law to carry a gun . . . and that you need a special permit just to own one?'

Latigo laughed again, but this time he didn't sound so confident. 'Even if that's true, which I doubt,' he said, 'it'll never happen out here. Not in the west. Folks wouldn't stand for it.'

★   ★   ★

Inside the store, several hard-looking men were drinking jug-whiskey at the bar. Four others played poker at a table in the corner. Two half-breed women wearing gun-belts stood talking at the sales counter while they waited for the owner, a balding, dour-faced man named Ed Hix, to collect their supplies from the shelves.

They paused and looked at the door as Gabe, Liberty and Drifter entered. Not recognizing them, the women became suspicious and their hands strayed to their six-guns. One of them, a big raw-boned brunette battling forty, excused herself and walked over to the poker table. She whispered in the ear of one player, who immediately turned and sized up the newcomers.

He frowned at Gabe for a moment, trying to place him; then as it hit him, he grinned and got to his feet. 'Mesquite?' he said, approaching Gabe. 'Mesquite Jennings, is that truly you?'

'In the flesh,' Gabe replied, extending

his hand. 'It's been a spell, *mi amigo.*'

'Four maybe five years,' the man said, shaking hands. 'Juarez, right?'

'*La Cotorra Verde.*'

'Goddamn,' the man said. 'You got one hell of a memory.'

''Cept when it comes to names,' Gabe replied. 'Jarod or Jason, wasn't it?'

'Mason,' the man corrected. 'Mason Parish.'

Gabe grinned. 'Sure. Now I remember. You ran with the Garret brothers out of El Paso. How they doing anyway?'

Parish shook his head. 'Feet up, both of 'em.'

'That's too bad. How'd it happen?'

'They got caught robbing a bank in Laredo.'

'The hell, you say.'

'They managed to shoot their way out, but killed a Pinkerton as they ran for their horses. It bought 'em a short trial and a long rope.'

'Damn,' Gabe said. 'Getting harder and harder to make a living.'

'Amen, brother.' Mason eyed Drifter and Liberty, adding: 'You running with these two now?'

'Them and two more outside. You might know one of 'em: Latigo Rawlins?'

'The bounty hunter?'

'Former bounty hunter,' Gabe corrected. 'A Sheriff in Las Cruces tried to cheat him out of his reward money. Lat' shot him, cleaned out the safe and has been on the run ever since.'

Mason accepted the lie without question. 'Lawmen,' he said bitterly. 'They're bigger thieves than any bank-robber I ever knew. Only one I ever met who had a grain of honesty in him was Macahan down in El Paso.'

'You know Ezra?' Drifter said.

'Well enough to hope he never dogs my trail,' Mason said. ''Cause if'n he does, it'll be time for my wife to buy me a headstone.'

'Can't fault that logic,' Drifter agreed. Before he could continue, one of the poker players yelled out to

Mason, wanting to know if he was still in the game.

'Be right there,' Mason replied. He grinned at Gabe, wished him luck and hurried back to the table.

Gabe turned to the barkeep, a stubby, leathery old man whose white beard was stained yellow with snuff and who had a badly-deformed club foot.

'Three whiskeys, *compadre*.' He waited until the barkeep returned with their drinks and then stacked enough *pesos* on the bar to include a big tip.

The barkeep was no fool. Eyeing the *pesos* suspiciously, he said: 'What do you want, mister?'

'We're looking for a fella. A Mex. Most likely rode in with a woman.'

'Squaw or 'breed?'

'Neither. She's white and pretty as sin with hair the color of corn silk.'

'Sure, sure, I seen him,' the barkeep said. He spat snuff juice into an empty coffee can behind the bar, wiped his mouth on his sleeve before adding: '*El Espada*'s his name. Was in here offering to let anyone bed her, many times as they wanted for ten *pesos* a ride.'

'That's cheap for what they're getting,' Drifter said, trying to control his rage. 'Where is he now?'

'First cabin you come to 'cross from the dynamite shed.'

'Thanks.'

'He a friend of yourn?'

'Why do you ask?'

''Cause I got to tell you, mister, I've run up against some pretty mean scum-bucks in my time, but *El Espada*, he tops the list. Had a rope around that gal's neck and drug her 'long behind him like she wasn't fit to spit.'

'Sounds like him,' Gabe said. He gulped down his drink, hoping it would calm his anger. Drifter and Liberty did the same. Then all three started for the door. There, Drifter paused and looked back at the barkeep, saying: 'One last question.'

'Fire away.'

'If something was to happen to the Mex, who'd come after us?'

'Everybody.'

'Got a soft spot for him, huh?'

'You couldn't be farther from the truth. Fact is there ain't a one of us wouldn't be happy to see him dead.'

'Then?'

'Rules are rules, mister. If you want to hide out here, you got to swear to protect one another.'

'No matter the crime?'

'Don't mean a damn what you've done, mister. The law's seen fit to hunt you down for it. Otherwise you wouldn't be here. All that matters to us is you follow our rules or leave. Simple as that.'

30

Outside in the relentless heat the four of them untied their horses, mounted up and rode slowly toward the row of cabins half-hidden by trees.

'Speak to me, dammit,' Latigo exclaimed when no one said anything. 'What happened? Did anyone see the Mex?'

'He's holed up in that cabin,' Drifter said, pointing.

'My mom — is she still with him?' Raven asked anxiously.

'According to the bartender, yes,' Liberty replied.

'How we going to get her out of there without him shooting her?'

'We're still working on that.'

'But — '

'Don't worry, sprout,' Gabe assured Raven. 'We'll find a way.'

'When you do,' Latigo reminded him,

'remember that bastard is mine. And this time,' he growled at Drifter, 'don't try to play God when I go to put a goddamn slug in his belly.'

'You keep that Colt leathered till I say so,' Liberty barked. 'I'm still running this circus, remember?'

Just then the door of the first cabin opened and two men stepped out. One of them was *El Espada* and the other, a younger man whose back was turned to them, was telling him something. Though they couldn't hear the conversation, by the young man's gesturing it was obvious he was giving the bandit leader orders.

When he was finished, he turned to mount his horse, revealing his face for the first time.

'Son of a bitch,' Drifter breathed. 'I should've known who was behind all this!'

'You know him?' Liberty whispered.

'We all do,' Gabe said through clenched teeth. 'That's Old Man Stadtlander's gutless, mealy-mouthed son, Slade!'

'What the hell's he doing here,' Latigo hissed, 'with that goddamn Mex?'

'Don't make sense,' Raven began.

'Sure it does,' Drifter said. 'Now that we know Stadtlander is involved, it makes all the sense in the world!'

Before anyone could ask why, both Slade and *El Espada* caught sight of them. Instantly recognizing Drifter, Gabe and Latigo, the two men dived for cover.

Latigo drew and fired a shot at *El Espada*. But fast as he was, he wasn't fast enough. The bandit leader scrambled safely back into the cabin, Latigo's bullet splintering the door behind him.

Slade, hidden by his rearing horse, dropped to one knee and fired at Drifter and the others. A moment later, *El Espada* started shooting at them through a rifle-slit in the shuttered window.

With bullets zipping about their heads Drifter, Gabe, Liberty, Latigo and Raven quickly sprinted for the nearby trees.

Slade and *El Espada* continued to blast away at them.

Ducked low, the five made it safely to the trees, bullets shredding the leaves all around them. Once they were behind cover, Liberty glared angrily at Latigo.

'Damn you, Lat! I told you to keep that iron leathered!'

'Guess I forgot, Marshal.'

His grin infuriated her. 'I don't believe that for a second. You just better hope nothing happens to Mrs. Bjorkman, or I'll see you swing for it!'

'Just try,' Latigo said. 'You'd end up spitting lead 'fore you even got your rope uncoiled.'

'Save your threats, both of you,' Drifter barked at them. 'We need clear heads if we're going to get Ingrid safely out of there.'

Liberty glared at Latigo for another tense moment and then turned to her father. 'You're right,' she said, calming. 'Shame on me. I was taught better than that — ' She suddenly winced, grunting painfully as a bullet slammed her against a tree.

Alarmed, Drifter moved quickly to her side. 'Where're you hit?'

Liberty indicated her left arm and gingerly unbuttoned her shirt.

'Let me see that.'

'Forget it, Daddy. It's just a graze.'

Ignoring her protests, Drifter gently peeled the left side of her shirt back until it was off her shoulder, revealing blood seeping from a bullet hole in her arm.

'Bullet went right through,' he said after examining the wound. 'You're lucky.'

'No, *lucky* people don't get shot — ' Her voice faded as she passed out.

'Emily.' Drifter patted her cheeks. 'Emily, can you hear me?'

Liberty opened her eyes and looked about her, trying to focus. 'Oh, God,' she groaned, embarrassed. 'Don't tell me I actually fainted.'

'Natural reaction,' her father said.

'Happens to everyone.'

Liberty glared at him. 'Daddy, don't make it worse by patronizing me.'

'How 'bout I stop the bleeding instead? Would that be okay?'

Liberty scowled, ready to blast him, and then saw his grin and had to laugh. 'Damn,' she said. 'Marshal Thompson's right. I really am an egregious pain in the ass, aren't I?'

'Could be,' Drifter said. Drawing his knife, he slit her sleeve, tore it into two strips and began wrapping her arm. 'That's if I knew what egregious meant.'

'There you go again,' she chided, 'playing that 'dumb cowboy' routine. When are you going to realize that it doesn't work on me?'

If Drifter heard her, he didn't show it. Knotting the makeshift bandage, he said: 'There, that ought to hold you until we can get you to a doctor.'

'Thanks. I — ' She broke off as Gabe joined them behind the tree.

'I'm all right,' she assured him as he

looked concerned. 'Just got winged is all.'

'Good. 'Cause we got other troubles.' Gabe thumbed in the direction of the general store. 'They're making plans to gun us down.'

Drifter and Liberty looked at the Comancheros and other armed outlaws that had gathered outside the store.

'Reckon the barkeep was right,' Drifter said. 'They do stick together.'

'I never doubted you,' Gabe said. Then to Liberty: ''Bout the only hope we got is to rush Slade and *El Espada* and barricade ourselves inside that cabin.'

'Temporary at best,' she replied. 'I mean, even if we were to make it there alive and managed to hold them off for a day or two — then what?'

'She's right,' Drifter said. 'It's not like the cavalry's on its way to rescue us.' He paused as Latigo came hurrying toward them.

Slade and *El Espada* also saw Latigo and started firing at him. Latigo ducked between trees as he ran, making himself a difficult target, and was winded by the time he finally reached Drifter and the others.

'R-Raven's gone,' he panted. 'I tried to g-grab her, but she ran off.'

'Little fool,' Liberty said. 'How does she think she's going to get into that cabin all by herself?'

'I don't think she intends to try,' Latigo said.

'What makes you say that?' Drifter asked.

''Cause she took off in the opposite direction.' He thumbed at the old, rundown shed marked DANGER that was built against the hillside near an abandoned mine entrance. 'That way.'

'Why there?' began Gabe and then stopped as Raven now emerged from the shed holding a small bundle in her arms. 'Wait! Look! There she is.'

'What the hell's she carrying?' Liberty said.

'Dynamite,' Drifter said grimly.

'Damn her hide,' cursed Latigo.

'She's going to get us all killed!'

Just then the men gathered outside the store also spotted Raven. On seeing the dynamite and guessing what she intended to do, they began shooting at her.

Alarmed, Raven started running, zigzagging to avoid the bullets kicking up dust about her feet.

Drifter, doubtful that she'd make it, opened fire at the men outside the store, forcing them to scatter and find cover.

Liberty, Gabe and Latigo joined in and together they kept the men pinned down while Raven sprinted toward the trees. At the same time Drifter kept an eye on Slade and *El Espada* in the cabin to make sure they didn't sneak out and find a clearing from where they could shoot her.

He needn't have worried. Raven quickly reached the safety of the trees and joined the foursome. As she leaned back against a tree to regain her breath, Gabe took the coiled length of safety fuse and bundle of dynamite sticks from her and cautiously set them down. 'What the devil were you thinking of?' he scolded. 'Are you trying to commit suicide? Hell, you could've been blown to bits if one of those bullets had hit its mark.'

'But they didn't, did they?'

'That still doesn't excuse what you did.'

'Well, somebody had to do something,' Raven grumbled, 'else we won't ever get Momma back.'

'Maybe,' said Drifter. 'But dynamite's not the answer. Those cliffs are too unstable. We start tossing explosives around and we could all end up getting buried along with the Comancheros.'

'You and your mom included,' Liberty said. 'Then what've we achieved?'

'Don't worry, that'll never happen,' Raven said confidently. 'See, I got this plan . . . '

31

Hidden among the trees, Drifter took an old gray shirt that countless washes had bleached almost white from his saddlebag, tied it to a branch and held it up. 'What do you think?' he asked the others. 'Reckon they'll know it's a flag of truce?'

'You'll soon find out,' Latigo said grimly, 'if lead starts flying.'

'Promise me one thing, Daddy,' Liberty said. 'If one of those *pendejos* even looks like he's reaching for his gun, shoot him and take cover, will you?'

'Nobody's going to slap leather,' Gabe assured her. 'Not so long as I'm holding this baby.' He held up a stick of dynamite. 'Hell, once I light the fuse, they know they only got a few seconds to give us their answer or else we all go up in smoke!'

'Unless they think we're bluffing,' Drifter said. 'Then all bets are off.'

'No, they ain't,' Raven snapped. 'Goddlemighty, didn't you listen to *anything* I told you?'

Amused by her bossiness, Drifter said: 'We wait them out?'

'Definitely.'

'What if they don't blink first?'

'They will.'

'Easy for you to say, young'un,' Latigo said. 'You ain't holding the dynamite.'

'I offered to,' she said. 'Not my fault if Mr. Longley wouldn't let me.'

She looked at Drifter for confirmation and he fondly ruffled her hair. 'Ignore Mr. Rawlins, sprout,' he said patiently. 'He's just trying to rattle your spurs. Now, be a good girl and hand me that fuse wire and two more sticks of dynamite.'

'What do you need those for?' Liberty asked anxiously.

'Insurance,' he replied, tucking the fuse and sticks into his shirt pocket. 'It isn't likely, but one of those yahoos might just be *loco* enough to think by shooting Gabe, he can snuff out the fuse before it sets off the dynamite.'

'Thanks,' Gabe said. 'That little gem of information is most reassuring.'

Drifter ignored him. 'Hopefully,' he continued to Liberty, 'when they see I got dynamite too, nobody'll try anything.'

'Now why didn't I think of that?' Raven grumbled.

'You thought of plenty,' Drifter assured her. 'And when this is over and your ma knows it was your plan that saved her, she's going to be mighty proud of you.' He gave her a fond squeeze. Then winking at Liberty, who managed a tentative smile in return, he and Gabe started toward the general store.

At first the denseness of the trees gave them cover. But as they neared the store the trees thinned out, affording them no protection from the Comancheros' guns.

Drifter and Gabe stopped behind the last tree. They were now less than twenty paces from the store. Ahead was nothing but open ground.

Drifter took out a match. 'Ready?' he asked Gabe.

'As I'll ever be.'

Drifter flared the match and held it under the fuse buried in the dynamite.

'Dammit, hold it still,' he grumbled as Gabe's hand shook.

'I *am* holding it still,' Gabe insisted. 'It's you that's shak — '

Suddenly the fuse caught fire and rapidly burned its way toward the dynamite.

'Jesus!' Drifter nipped out the fuse. 'That would've exploded way too soon.'

'We need another plan,' Gabe said.

'Or a longer fuse. Here, you take this.' Drifter handed Gabe the flag then cut off a length of fuse and inserted it into the dynamite. 'I'll do the rest.'

'Be my guest,' Gabe said happily.

'Just one thing: while we're walking,

don't forget to keep waving the flag.'

'Yeah, yeah, yeah.'

'I'm serious. If you don't wave it, they'll shoot us.'

'I'll wave it, I'll wave it, for chrissake!'

'No need to get your bowels in an uproar.'

'Then quit nagging me.'

'Who's nagging? I'm just making sure everything goes smoothly is all.'

'Trust me, it will. Hell, I may not be the smartest bear in the woods but give me *some* credit.' Before Drifter could reply, Gabe stepped from behind the tree and began waving the flag at the Comancheros.

Drifter quickly joined him and lit another match. Holding the flame under the fuse, but not close enough for it to catch fire, he told Gabe to start walking.

Gabe obeyed. Together, they slowly approached the store.

'*Que pasa?*' an old Comanchero demanded. 'What you want, *gringos?*'

'To talk,' Drifter replied.

'Talk? We no talk. What we talk about?'

'What the hell do think?' Gabe exclaimed. 'Releasing the woman!'

'We let woman go, *gringo* — only when you pay ten thousand in gold!'

'That ain't going to happen,' Gabe said. 'Not now, not ever.'

'Then no need to make talk,' the old Comanchero replied.

'That's too bad,' Drifter said, holding the match flame closer to the fuse. 'Because that means you end up with nothing. Not even your lives.'

'Go ahead, *gringo*, light it,' jeered another Comanchero. 'With short fuse like that, you die with us.'

'That's for true,' agreed Drifter. 'Difference is that woman's family and without her, we don't care if we live or die.'

The Comanchero laughed, spat at Drifter's feet and said something derogatory to his companions. They all roared with laughter.

Drifter casually lit the fuse. It sizzled

and started burning. Drifter extended his free hand to Gabe, saying: 'See you in the hereafter, *amigo.*'

'Looking forward to it,' said Gabe, shaking hands.

He and Drifter calmly watched as the fuse burned its way toward the dynamite.

The Comancheros stopped laughing. They stared uneasily at the burning fuse, anxiously biting their lips.

'*Si conoces a ninguna oracions,*' Gabe said, '*ahora es el momento de decirles.*'

The mention of prayers made the Comancheros even more anxious.

'*Señor,*' the old Comanchero replied, 'there is no need to pray. What you do, it is not — how you say?'

'Necessary?' Gabe suggested.

'*Si, si* . . . necessary. First you put out fuse, *por favor*, then we talk.'

'No,' Drifter said firmly. '*First*, you get the woman. *Muy pronto!*'

Angry murmurs arose from the Comancheros.

Drifter didn't wilt.

There was now only an inch of unlit fuse left.

The old Comanchero stared nervously at it, wetted his lips and . . . blinked.

'You win, *señor*. I do like you ask. Get woman.'

'*Bueno*!' Drifter said, eying the burning fuse. 'Better hurry, though, 'cause we're all about one minute from hell.'

'*Si, si*, I hurry.' He ran off.

Drifter turned to Gabe. 'Light another match, *amigo*, and give it to me the moment I snub out the fuse.'

'Good thinking,' Gabe said. 'I don't trust these coyotes either.'

Drifter waited until Gabe had flared a match before pinching out the fuse. He then held Gabe's match under the remaining inch of fuse and turned back to the Comancheros. They glared at him, weapons clenched, itching to kill him.

'Get ready to light another match,'

Drifter told Gabe. 'I don't want these 'breeds getting any ideas about shooting me once this flame goes out.'

Gabe nodded and took out a handful of matches. Keeping two, he returned the rest to his shirt pocket. He then stuck one match between his teeth and prepared to light the other with his thumbnail.

It wasn't necessary. The old Comanchero now emerged from the first cabin. With him were *El Espada* and Ingrid. She had rope burns around her neck, her clothes were torn and her hair a tangled mess. There were also bruises on her face, showing she'd been beaten. But the fearless, determined look in her eyes proved she was not defeated.

By now the match in Drifter's hand was flickering, ready to go out. Beside him, Gabe scratched the match he was holding with his thumbnail. The flame flared and he handed the match to Drifter, who held it under the dynamite fuse.

The old Comanchero now confronted Drifter. Indicating Ingrid, who stood between him and *El Espada*, he said: 'See, *jefe*, I bring her like you say.'

Drifter, noticing that *El Espada* was holding Ingrid's hair, said: 'Tell him to let her go, Gabe.'

Gabe spoke in Spanish to *El Espada*. The bandit leader gave a sneering laugh and cruelly tightened his hold on Ingrid's hair, making her wince.

Drifter immediately held the flame close to the fuse.

'You not frighten me, *gringo*,' *El Espada* snarled. 'You no harm your woman.'

Drifter turned to Ingrid. 'I need to know something.'

'What?'

'Given a choice, would you sooner live and be with this bastard . . . or die?'

'Die,' she replied instantly.

'You heard the lady,' Drifter told *El Espada*. 'Now let her go.'

'*Nunca!*'

'Did he just say 'never'?' Drifter asked Gabe.

''Fraid so.'

Drifter turned to the bandit leader. 'I'm going to ask you one more time. Hand over the woman.'

'*Nunca*,' *El Espada* repeated. 'I shoot this bitch 'fore I let you have her, *hijo de puta*!'

'Do me a favor,' Ingrid said to Drifter. 'When I'm dead, kill him.'

'With pleasure.'

'Hold it,' Gabe said as Drifter prepared to draw. 'Let me handle this.'

'Why you?'

'She's my woman.' Gabe waited for Drifter to step aside and then faced *El Espada*, hand poised above his Colt. 'Last chance, *culero*!'

El Espada released Ingrid, and grabbed for his gun.

It was close. But Gabe cleared leather first. Fired.

The bullet punched a hole in *El Espada*'s chest. He staggered back and stood there, motionless, eyes wide with shock, still holding his half-drawn gun, blood welling from the wound above his heart. Then slowly his legs buckled and he collapsed on his face.

Gabe flipped the body over with the toe of his boot.

El Espada glared at him. His lips worked with great effort. Gabe knelt down and put his ear to the Mexican's mouth. *El Espada* whispered something and died.

'What'd he say?' Drifter asked Gabe.

'It loses something in the translation.'

'Tell me anyway.'

'Something about, when he meets Slade in hell, he's going to kill him.'

'I thought they were partners?'

'They were. But apparently Slade cheated him out of the money he was promised.'

Drifter shook his head in disgust. He then held up the stick of dynamite to the old Comanchero, saying: 'If your men try to stop us from leaving, I'll light this.'

'Your message is clear, *señor*.' The

old Comanchero stepped up into the saddle and motioned for the other Comancheros to get mounted. '*Vaya con Dios.*'

'*Vaya con Dios,*' Drifter said. He waited until the Comancheros had ridden off and then turned to Gabe and Ingrid. 'I hope he's right.'

'About what?' Ingrid asked.

'God riding with us.'

32

At the border Gabe said goodbye to Ingrid and Raven, promising to see them again soon, and then joined Drifter, Latigo and Liberty who were waiting by their horses.

'Make sure they get home safely,' he said to Drifter. 'Stadtlander's going to be one unhappy fella when he finds out that Ingrid's no longer *El Espada*'s prisoner.'

'He's going to be even more unhappy when I charge his son with kidnapping,' Liberty said grimly.

'Can't you charge the old man, too?' Latigo said. 'I mean we all know he was behind this. Slade doesn't have the guts to take a piss without getting his pa's permission.'

'I'll do my best,' Liberty promised. 'But unless Slade wants to snitch on his father, which I doubt, it'll be almost impossible to prove he had a hand in it.'

'Well, at least try,' Gabe said. 'Even if you can't nail his hide to the court-house door, it'd be fun watching him sweat a little.'

'Amen to that,' said Latigo. Then to Drifter: 'Listen, I've been thinking, Ace. I got nothing pressing to do up north, so I think I'll stay down here for a spell — maybe get into some trouble with Gabe. That okay with you?'

'Sure. Soon as I get Ingrid and Raven settled, I'll be heading back to the ranch anyway. There's plenty of stuff needs fixing and come spring, there'll be a whole bunch of new calves and foals to tend to.'

'Fine. Maybe next time I'm in or around El Paso, I'll hit you up for a beer.'

'Be my pleasure. So long, Lefty. Take care of yourself.'

'Always,' said Latigo. He grinned at Liberty. 'Look after your old man, Marshal. He's getting a bit long in the tooth.' He was gone before Drifter could find a suitable retort.

★ ★ ★

It didn't take long to reach the Bjorkman spread. Drifter watered their horses while Liberty made sure that Ingrid and Raven were safely settled in, and then he and his daughter continued on to Stadtlander's ranch.

It was an hour's ride to the high, arched, signature gateway that warned riders they were entering Double S land; and then a twenty-minute climb up to the crest of the grassy, flat-topped knoll on which stood Stillman J. Stadtlander's impressive, western-style mansion and surrounding corrals and outbuildings.

Drifter and Liberty reined in their sweat-caked horses as they reached the gated area fronting the mansion. One of several tough-looking ranch-hands confronted them at the gate. He made no attempt to be friendly. But he knew better than to argue with Liberty's badge and opening the gate, escorted them to the front porch. There, as they dismounted, they spotted another hand ducking into a side-door.

'Reckon we're being announced,' Drifter said.

'Think we'll be invited for lunch?' Liberty asked wryly.

'Only if they're serving sidewinder stew.'

Despite themselves, they both chuckled. Then removing their hats, they slapped the trail dust from their clothes and started up the front steps.

'Watch yourself, Emily,' Drifter warned. 'Stadtlander coils when he sits.'

'Don't worry, Daddy. I've dealt with snakes before.'

The door, a heavy slab of oak with the familiar Double S brand ornately carved on it, swung open as they stepped onto the wide veranda-styled porch, and a well-groomed rancher in his late sixties limped out. Though he was short, stumpy and hampered by arthritis, his jut-jawed face, defiant steely gaze, pugnacious chin and thin-lipped mouth warned everyone that Stillman J. Stadtlander was an adversary to be avoided at all costs. He walked carefully, not trusting his legs to support him, angrily swatting away the arm that his servant offered him, relying instead on a silver-handled mahogany walking stick.

'Mr. Standtlander,' Liberty began, 'I'm — '

'I know who you are, Deputy,' Stadtlander snapped. 'State your damn' business and then get the hell off my property.'

'Haven't lost any of your charm, I see,' Drifter drawled.

'And you're still hanging around lawmen,' Stadtlander replied. 'So I guess neither of us has changed.' Turning back to Liberty, he added: 'I told you to state your business, girl.'

Liberty flushed angrily. 'I'm a Deputy US Marshal, Mr. Stadtlander, not a girl. And even if old age has made you blind as well as rude, this badge I'm wearing says you'll treat me with the respect I deserve.'

'And if I don't?' he said, testing her.

'Then I'll find a reason to arrest you and keep you locked up in jail until the circuit judge arrives. And we all know how long that can take, don't we — *sir?*'

For a moment Stadtlander seemed about to explode. His fleshy, belligerent face went purple, veins bulged in his temples, and his hands balled into fists.

Beside him his white-coated servant took a half-step backward, as if not wanting to be within range of those fists — which, he sensed, at any moment would need to punch someone.

Several cowhands working near the porch also recoiled, and two of them started toward the nearest corral where their gun-belts hung.

Seeing them out the corner of his eye Drifter dropped his hand to his Colt, turned and froze the men with a thin lethal smile that Latigo would have envied.

Then a strange thing happened: Stadtlander recovered his poise, the anger drained from his face and he looked at Liberty with a sort of belligerent respect.

'Why don't you come inside, Deputy? You look like you've ridden a far piece and could use something cool to drink.'

'That would be nice,' Liberty said politely. 'The ride up from the border has made Mr. Longley and me awfully thirsty.' She moved to the door, which the servant politely opened for her, and entered a large oak-paneled hall that smelled of brandy and expensive cigars. She stood there waiting for Drifter to join her.

'Lemonade,' Stadtlander barked at the servant. Then to Liberty: 'We'll talk in my study.' He led the way, limping under a fancy chandelier to big double doors at the rear of the foyer.

'You have a magnificent home,' Liberty said, looking around. 'You must be very proud.'

Stadtlander frowned, saddened by memories, and said bitterly: 'I was — once.'

'I don't understand.'

'I built it for my wife. When she passed, it became less important to me. Then later, when my daughter died . . . ' His voice sadly trailed off.

'I'm sorry,' Liberty said. 'I had no idea. Losing one's family . . . is something one never really gets over.' She glanced at Drifter as she spoke and though there was no resentment in her eyes, he felt a stab of guilt.

Stadtlander's study took up a whole corner of the mansion. The large oak-paneled room had windows on two sides, one facing the scrubland on which his vast herd grazed and the other offering a panoramic view of the distant Rio Grande. Western paintings and deer and elk trophy heads adorned the walls and grizzly pelts lay on the stained-wood floor.

The massive furniture was covered in brown-and-white cowhide and there was enough room in the giant stone fireplace to spit-roast a whole steer. Above it hung an imposing oil painting of Stadtlander astride a black Morgan stallion, posed like an empire-builder, while facing him across the room hung an equally impressive painting of his deceased wife, Agatha. A pale, delicate, sweet-faced easterner of obvious fine breeding, she seemed misplaced in this testosterone-filled atmosphere. Hanging beside her were smaller portraits of Slade and his dead sister, Elizabeth, both in their early teens.

Stadtlander limped behind a hand-hewn bar that stretched along one entire wall and poured himself a tumbler of J.H. Cutter.

'While I'm waiting for the lemonade,' Liberty said, 'I could use one of those.'

'So could I,' said Drifter. 'That's if you're offering?'

Stadtlander poured two more whiskeys and set them on the bar in front of them.

'All right,' he said aggressively, 'we've

wasted enough time on pleasantries, Deputy, so now tell me why you're here.'

Liberty took a drink, felt the whiskey glide smoothly down her parched throat and felt better. 'I think you already know the reason, Mr. Stadtlander. But just to make it official: to arrest your son, Slade.'

'For what reason, dammit?'

'Kidnapping and illegally transporting the victim, Mrs. Ingrid Bjorkman, across the border into Mexico.'

Stadtlander gave a raspy chuckle, drained his drink and poured himself another. 'The hell you say.' He took a gulp and slammed the tumbler down so hard the whiskey splashed onto the bar. 'You got sand, Deputy, I'll give you that. But do you truly think I'm going to turn my boy over to you on some trumped-up charge that any sane judge will toss out of court?'

'These charges, sir, are not trumped up. I personally brought Mrs. Bjorkman and her daughter back from Mexico.'

'So? What's that got to do with my boy? I mean, did this Bjorkman woman accuse Slade of kidnapping her?'

'You know damn well she didn't,' put in Drifter. 'Slade doesn't have the spine to actually commit a crime himself. Like you, he pays someone else to do his dirty work — pays, I might add, with your money.'

Stadtlander ignored Drifter and said to Liberty: 'You have proof of this, Deputy? The kidnapper himself, perhaps?'

'No.'

'A live witness, then? Someone willing to swear in court that my boy hired him to kidnap Mrs. Bjorkman?'

'You know I don't, sir.'

'Oh, and how would I know that?'

'From Slade,' Drifter said, unable to keep quiet any longer.

Again Stadtlander ignored him. 'Am I to assume your witness is dead?' he asked Liberty.

'Yes.'

'Well, I know you're new at this,

Deputy, but even you should know that a dead witness doesn't hold much sway in court — not in these United States of America!'

Liberty, keeping her temper under wraps, said: 'I'm not interested in what dead witnesses can or cannot do, Mr. Stadtlander. All I want is for you to fetch your son, now, or I will charge you with obstructing justice and arrest you in his place.'

Stadtlander lost his fake smile. 'You actually think you could do that, Deputy? Arrest me, Stillman J. Stadtlander, and march me out of my own house in front of my men — all fifty-two of them — without anyone trying to stop you?'

'If she can't,' Drifter said, drawing his Colt and resting it on the bar, 'I can.'

'Mr. Longley,' Liberty began. 'You don't have to defend — '

'No, no, let him speak,' Stadtlander insisted. 'I'm sure my lawyers will enjoy repeating every threat he makes to Judge Hartley — the same Judge Hartley, I might remind you, whose only daughter, Stephanie, became betrothed in this very room on this very ranch, not more than six months ago!'

Liberty swallowed hard and tried not to be intimidated. 'For the last time, sir, will you turn your son over to me or not?'

Stadtlander glared defiantly at her, but said nothing.

Tired of the rancher's stalling, Drifter picked up his Colt, spun the cylinder on his forearm, cocked the hammer and aimed it at the belligerent rancher. 'Do like she says, you pompous, arrogant blowhard!'

Stadtlander paled but to his credit, stood his ground. 'And if I don't, Deputy, are you going to stand by while this known troublemaker shoots me in cold blood?'

'Put your gun away, Mr. Longley,' Liberty told Drifter. She waited until he grudgingly obeyed and then turned back to Stadtlander. 'As for you, sir, I'm placing you under arrest for willfully obstructing justice.' She unhooked her handcuffs from her belt, adding: 'Now, turn around and put your hands behind your back.'

For a moment Stadtlander stared in utter disbelief at her. Then he broke into hearty laughter, gulped down his drink, said: 'Wait here, Deputy, while I fetch my boy.' He set his glass down and before Liberty could argue, limped from the room.

Liberty turned to Drifter. 'Daddy, if you ever threaten anyone in front of me again, I swear I'll arrest you, lock you in the hoosegow and throw away the damn' key!'

Drifter looked at his daughter and tried not to laugh. ''Hoosegow'?' he croaked. 'Did you just say 'hoosegow'? My God, Emily, when the hell did *you* start reading dime novels?'

33

Drifter and Liberty, with Slade hand-cuffed between them, entered the Sheriff's office and found Lonnie Forbes dozing behind his desk. A big fleshy man in his early fifties with thinning gray hair and a gunfighter's mustache, he sat leaned back in his chair, leathery hands clasped across his ample belly, his loud snoring and fluttering lips keeping several circling flies from landing on his face.

Drifter deliberately slammed the door, waking the Sheriff with a start. The big lawman almost lost his balance as the chair tipped backward, while his long legs slid off the desk . . . pens, papers and wanted posters cascading to the floor.

'Dammit,' he said, blinking owlishly at them, 'don't you know better than to wake a fella up like that? You could give a body a seizure!'

'Santa Rosa ain't that lucky,' Drifter said.

The Sheriff ignored him and after giving Slade a troubled look, said to Liberty: 'You got business with me, Deputy?'

'Yes. I want to leave my prisoner here overnight. I'm taking him to Deming on the morning train and I'll feel safer if he's behind bars.'

Sheriff Forbes picked up the spilled papers and put them on his desk, the effort making him grunt, and got to his feet. He was as tall as Drifter, but outweighed him by fifty pounds, and every movement brought more sweat to his forehead.

'What're the charges, Deputy?'

'Kidnapping, for one.'

'It's a goddamned lie,' Slade snarled. 'I had nothing to do with grabbing that Bjorkman woman, or taking her across the border.'

'Ingrid Bjorkman was kidnapped?' the Sheriff said with exaggerated surprise. 'By God, that's the first I've heard of it.'

'You're a liar, Lonnie,' Drifter said. 'You not only knew about it, but you were in on it all along. You *and* Stillman Stadtlander. He planned it, paid for it and then had you, his pet weasel pay *El Espada* to do his dirty work!'

'You're *loco*,' Forbes said. 'Why would Mr. Stadtlander want to kidnap Mrs. Bjorkman?'

'As bait,' Drifter said, 'to draw me and Gabe Moonlight away from her ranch.'

'I'm confused,' Forbes said. 'Why would he care if you two were there or not?'

''Cause Stadtlander owns the deed to Ingrid's spread. Bought it from the bank some time back.'

'What's that got to do with — ?'

'Shut up and listen!'

'You can't talk to me like — ' The Sheriff stopped as Drifter drew his Colt, thumbed the hammer back and pressed the muzzle against Forbes' forehead.

'Feel like listening now, you fat tub of lard?'

235

Alarmed, Sheriff Forbes nodded and fresh sweat beaded on his forehead.

'There's a clause in the note,' Drifter said, holstering his gun, 'that says if Ingrid defaults on the loan or the property is left unattended — no matter the reason — the place can be taken over by the deed holder. Now that may not be the actual legal wording, but it's close enough for you to get my drift.'

'I didn't know this,' Forbes said.

'Well, you know it now.'

'Yes, but . . . I still don't see why you think I'm involved in this. I certainly don't hold the note, as you just pointed out, and I got no interest in living out there — '

'I know that,' Drifter said. 'But you're Stadtlander's puppet, which means you jump when he pulls your strings, and you've been spending time at the Double S lately — '

'So?'

'So Stadtlander needed someone to pay *El Espada* to kidnap Ingrid and you fitted the bill.'

Stung by the accusation, the Sheriff said angrily: 'You finished?'

'You know I ain't.'

'Then get to the meat.'

'Gladly. I was in Palomas recently — around the same time you were paying off *El Espada*.'

'That's a lie, but go on.'

'I figure you must've seen me. You must've also thought I saw you.'

'What makes you say that?'

''Cause that's why you followed me, put two rounds in my back and left me for dead just outside of town. But unfortunately for you, I don't die easy and — '

The Sheriff, sweating profusely, stopped him. 'You got any proof to back up all this, Quint? Or are you just flapping your gums to sound like a big man before your daughter, here?'

'He don't have one shred of proof,' Slade blurted. 'Against you or me!'

There was silence save for the flies buzzing against the window.

'That's where you're wrong,' Drifter

237

said quietly. He took something from his pocket and opened his fingers to show two slugs and two spent rifle cartridge casings in his palm.

'What're those?' Forbes asked uneasily.

'You should know,' Drifter said, ignoring Liberty's surprised look. 'They were fired from your Henry.'

Forbes looked even more uneasy. 'I — I don't own a Henry,' he stammered.

'That's another lie.'

'Prove it.'

'I intend to.' Drifter went to the gun rack standing against the nearby wall. Three Winchester model '91s and two 12-gauge shotguns were locked in the first five slots. The sixth and last slot was — empty.

Drifter turned to the Sheriff, demanding: 'Where the hell is it, Lonnie?'

'Where's what?'

'That old Henry repeater you always keep right here?' He thumbed at the empty slot.

'Oh, *that*.' Sheriff Forbes shrugged

with exaggerated innocence. 'Sorry to disappoint you, Quint, but that rifle's been missing for what — six months at least. Stolen right out of that rack one day when I was at lunch. Damned shame, too. I always had a hankering for that gun.'

'And naturally, you never found out who stole it?' Drifter said sarcastically.

'Never did, no.'

'Most likely it was the same fella that put them two slugs in your back,' Slade said to Drifter. 'Oh, and 'fore you ask me how I knew that, Mr. Longley, sir, you just mentioned it. And even if you hadn't, I heard Lars Gustavson talking about it over at the livery.'

'When would that be?' Drifter said.

'Sorry, I can't remember,' Slade smirked. 'Remembering dates has always been a problem for me ever since I was a young'un.'

'I got a cure for that,' Drifter said, his tone menacing. 'I take you out back and beat you bloody until your memory returns and — '

The door opened, startling them. In

walked a small, bulky, balding man in an expensive western-styled suit, immaculate tan Stetson and a black string tie who exuded an air of self-importance.

Drifter didn't recognize him, but it was obvious everyone else did because they all respectfully straightened up.

Ignoring them, the man confronted the Sheriff and wagged a judicial finger in his face. 'Have you arrested Mr. Slade Stadtlander yet?' he demanded.

'No, judge,' Forbes said. 'But I was about to lock him up.'

'On whose authority, may I ask?'

'Mine, Judge Hartley,' Liberty said.

'On what charge, Deputy?'

'Kidnapping, Your Honor.'

'She's lying,' Slade blurted. 'I didn't kidnap nobody. And I didn't *pay* nobody to kidnap anyone neither. Ask my old man. He'll tell you, judge. Mr. Longley and this Marshal, here, they got it in for me and — '

'Be quiet!' Judge Hartley snapped. As Slade fell silent, the judge turned to Liberty, saying: 'I know your work,

240

Deputy, and I have great admiration for your integrity and respect for the law. But I must caution you, here, not to — how shall I say — put the wagon before the horse, so to speak.'

'What're you suggesting, Your Honor?'

'That you provide proof that Mr. Stadtlander did indeed kidnap Mrs — uhm — '

'Bjorkman,' Liberty said.

'Mrs. Bjorkman, before having him wrongfully incarcerated. Do you have that proof, Deputy?' he added sharply.

'How can she?' Slade chimed in. 'I never done nothing.'

'I told you to be quiet, young man.' Judge Hartley waited for Slade to subside, then turned to Liberty: 'Well, Deputy? Do you have that proof?'

Liberty took a long, deep breath. She wanted to lie and say yes but realized her career *and* her integrity were on the line. The price was too high and despite wanting to see justice prevail, she finally said: 'No, Your Honor. I do not.'

Judge Hartley beamed smugly and

turned to Lonnie Forbes. 'Do you have anything to add, Sheriff?'

'No, Your Honor.'

'Then unless anyone else has objections, I shall escort Mr. Stadtlander back to his father. Good day, everyone.' He hustled Slade out of the office, the door banging behind them.

Drifter sighed, and then winced as his ulcer flared up.

'Well,' Sheriff Forbes said to Liberty, 'I reckon that wraps things up, wouldn't you say, Deputy?'

'Yes,' she said, hoping she'd made the right choice. 'I would indeed.'

'Will you be returning to Guthrie now?'

'Yes. On the morning train.'

'Have a safe journey,' Sheriff Forbes said, trying not to gloat. 'And be sure to remember me to Marshal Thompson.'

Liberty nodded and walked to the door.

Drifter gave the Sheriff a chilling look. 'This ain't over, Lonnie. Not by a long shot.'

'Are you threatening me?' Sheriff Forbes said.

'What do you think?' Drifter said. Going to the door, he opened it for his daughter and together they walked out into the bright, hot, Santa Rosa sunlight.

34

It was one of those typical warm, gold-blue New Mexico mornings when Drifter and Liberty arrived at the train station. Drifter insisted on buying her ticket to Guthrie, Oklahoma, even though she explained that transportation came out of her travel expenses, and by the time they walked out onto the sun-dappled platform, a distant spiral of black smoke verified that the train was only minutes away.

'Will you be going back to El Paso tonight?' Liberty asked her father.

Drifter shook his head. 'Not for a few days, most likely.'

She frowned suspiciously at him. 'Daddy, you're not thinking of stirring things up around here, are you? And don't give me that 'who me?' look,' she added crossly. 'You're no better at pretending to be 'Mr. Innocent' than you are playing the 'dumb cowboy' act.'

'Got me pegged, have you?'

'After all the time we've spent together recently, I surely hope so.'

Drifter grinned, amused by her remark. But as he gave deeper thought to what she'd just said, as usual he felt guilty.

'I know raising cattle and horses ain't as exciting as being a Marshal,' he said, watching the train drawing ever closer. 'But I want you to know that having you around lately has made me mighty happy. And that's God's honest truth.'

Liberty smiled. 'Funny you should say that, Daddy. I was thinking the exact same thing.' She paused as a shrill whistle came from the approaching train and then said: 'We're so lucky, you and me.'

'We are?'

'Don't you think so?'

'Never really gave it much thought,' he lied.

'Well, I have. I think about it all the time. I mean, goodness me, who else do you know that's earning wages doing exactly what they want to do, with the person they want to do it with, and have the rest of their lives to enjoy doing it together? Does that make any sense?' she added, as if not sure herself.

Her father had no idea, but he said anyway: 'All the sense in the world.'

'You are such a liar, Daddy.' Liberty laughed, and standing on her toes kissed him on the cheek. 'But I love you anyway.'

Drifter swallowed the lump in his throat and was grateful that the train was almost to the station now.

'Would you do me a favor?' she asked.

'Sure. What?'

'I hate long goodbyes. So can we say goodbye now and then you leave — you know, before the train actually gets here?'

'If that's what you want, sure,' Drifter said thankfully.

'It is. So give me a big hug and get going, okay?'

Drifter wrapped his arms around his daughter and squeezed the breath out of her. Then he kissed her on the nose and pressed his cheek against hers, feeling wonderful at that moment. He then forced himself to let her go, stepped back and quickly walked toward the livery stable.

'G'bye,' he heard her call out. 'Love you, Daddy.'

Not daring to look around, or even answer, he gave a quick back-handed wave and continued walking.

Behind him, he could hear the shushing of the steam brakes as the train pulled into the station, felt the ground tremble as the heavy steel wheels ground to a stop, and then heard the cheerful chatter of arriving passengers.

Emily's right, he thought. We are lucky. Luckier than most. And even if my life ended today or tomorrow, or next month or whenever, I'd consider myself blessed.

It was then he heard shots being fired in the vicinity of the bank.

Screams and shouting followed.
Then . . . more and more gunshots.
Wondering if the bank was being robbed, Drifter drew his Colt and started running toward Main Street.

THE END

We do hope that you have enjoyed reading this large print book.

Did you know that all of our titles are available for purchase?

We publish a wide range of high quality large print books including:
Romances, Mysteries, Classics
General Fiction
Non Fiction and Westerns

Special interest titles available in large print are:
The Little Oxford Dictionary
Music Book, Song Book
Hymn Book, Service Book

Also available from us courtesy of Oxford University Press:
Young Readers' Dictionary
(large print edition)
Young Readers' Thesaurus
(large print edition)

For further information or a free brochure, please contact us at:
Ulverscroft Large Print Books Ltd.,
The Green, Bradgate Road, Anstey,
Leicester, LE7 7FU, England.
Tel: (00 44) **0116 236 4325**
Fax: (00 44) **0116 234 0205**

POWDER RIVER

Jack Edwardes

As the State Governor's lawmen spread throughout Wyoming, the days of the bounty hunter are coming to a close. For hired gun Brad Thornton, this spells the end of an era. The men in badges aren't yet everywhere, though, and rancher Moreton Frewen needs immediate action: rustlers are stealing his stock, and Thornton is just the man to make the culprits pay. But these are no run-of-the-mill cattle thieves. The Morgan gang are ruthless killers, prepared to turn their hands to anything from bank robbery to murder . . .